RECLINING NUDE

Reclining Nude

Claudia Riess

STEIN AND DAY/*Publishers*/New York

First published in 1982
Copyright ®1982 by Claudia Riess
All rights reserved
Designed by Lou Ditizio
Printed in the United States of America
STEIN AND DAY / *Publishers*
Scarborough House
Briarcliff Manor, N.Y. 10510

Library of Congress Cataloging in Publication Data

Riess, Claudia.
  Reclining nude.

    I. Title.
PS3568.I364R4   1982   813'.54   82-10589
ISBN 0-8128-2869-0

RECLINING NUDE

1

I sat on the beach, my third floor Lord and Taylor jeans rolled above my ankles, and tried to clear my mind of that checklist of chores that gave my life form without substance:

pick up mail — roll of stamps
call NY Times re pprs dumped puddles
trans savngs to chking to cover mtg, tel
switch John's D.D.S. appt to Tues (?)
Gristedes — mushrms, chkn, skim mlk
tell Bill's Meats to shove gamey London brl up ass
Hampton Stnry — ppr clips, bics, envlps

My little gold Omega, given to me by my mother-in-law and as faithful and predictable as her other gift, her son, read 11:30. There was time to do the shopping and calling before the kids came home from school. Screw it. Maybe it could wait for tomorrow. I stretched and stood up, brushed the sand from my jacket, and ambled closer to the ocean.

The March lamb was still shivering in the dune grass and the beach was empty, except for a few sandpipers. I, Joan Hiller, ex-child with potential and presently mother of two, stood at the water's edge and filled my lungs with clean ocean air. The cool

3

sand caressed my bare toes and I wiggled them as a gesture of communion.

Unlike in sex, when the intellect abdicates (or is supposed to) with the arousal of the senses, I fervently tried to interpret my heightened feelings and my fascination with the indifferent waves. The crisp wind tossed my hair against my cheeks and teased me into collegiate thoughts of existential being. (How long had it been since those demitasse evenings at Vassar, when the dilemmas of the universe were at the center of straining minds, and hours were spent in heated discussions over Sartre's transcendental ego and Husserl's noesis? Gone, gone were those sheltered evenings of bridge and passionate mentation!) I breathed in the smell of salt air and fishy things and, in a moment torn between exhilaration and frustration, cried out "Bullshit!" to the blue horizon.

It was a little past noon when I pulled into the gravel driveway of my split-level colonial in Hampton Village and put my VW into Park. The plan was to take a bath and shave my legs, and then drop by Harrison's Real Estate Agency, where I worked part time, to see if any new summer rentals were in the offing. (Another activity in a life of miscellanies. The job wasn't exactly definitive, but the small income allowed for big indulgences, especially around the holiday season.)

The phone was ringing as I entered the house (make note: white paint on door chipping) and I ran to answer it. It was Susan.

"Hi, Joan. What's new?"

Susan began all telephone conversations with "What's new?" and it was inevitable that no matter *what* was new, if anything, after that question I would lose all interest in communicating it. "Oh, nothing. How's Bobby? Send him back to school today?"

"I kept him home. He still seemed a little pale and lethargic."

It was hard to imagine. I had never seen Bobby in anything but a frenetic whirlwind—spinning, jumping, racing his dog, tearing into his brother.

Pulling the telephone cord to its full length, I reached into the refrigerator for the grapefruit juice, then the olive loaf (make note: stop eating crap). "Good idea."

"Want to go look at carpeting Wednesday? Weren't you thinking of re-doing your den? Maybe I'll finally do my bedroom."

"I don't think so. I'm not in a rug mood." My voice was muffled by a slice of olive loaf. "Screw my den."

"Gee, what's gotten into *you?*"

"Nothing, unfortunately."

"Joan!" (Both prudes—at least in deed, if not thought—but I could shoot my mouth off.)

There was the sound of a crash followed by a howl coming from Susan's house. Bobby must be emerging from his lassitude.

"Gotta run! I think something just broke!"

The phone clicked in my ear. Thoughts of my kids filled the void. I was still holding the receiver up to my ear.

Where were they now behind the red brick walls? Sitting at their desks? Laura, six, at this very moment reaching under her skirt to tug at her underpants? John, eight, dependent and forgetful—was he scrounging around looking for his eraser while his teacher was chalking through a mathematical concept? Was he missing the gist? I put back the receiver. A sudden pang of anxiety hit me like a uterine contraction. Those soft bits of life—they were so vulnerable! To the big school buses, and the hurtling cars, and all the hard staircases, and the meanness! Protect! I pressed down on the receiver, pressing away unmanageable fears. The moment passed.

I grabbed another slice of olive loaf and gulped down the juice. It felt like wine. I was giddy. I wrapped the remaining olive loaf in aluminum foil and put away the juice container. Everything in order.

I went up to my room to undress and prepare my bath.

As soon as my clothes were off, I stripped myself of worries, my list, Mr. Harrison's rentals, the pile of mail on my dresser, the unfolded underwear in the laundry basket, the chipped paint, the worn carpet. I listened to the water running in the tub, into which I had dumped a generous helping of bath gel, and lay on my bed, my legs spread wide.

There was nothing on my list about it, but it was essential. Desire.

I turned off the water. It was very hot and I went back to the bedroom to pick out some clean clothes while the water cooled off a little. Meanwhile, the pressure was mischievously building up between my legs. Every step I took seemed to provoke it.

I cupped my hands to my breasts and squeezed. Still a firm and healthy B's worth. What a pity so eager and hungry a body could have gone so long without a feast. Too bad early brainwashing and prudence had me lagging about ten years behind my generation—or at least its reputation. What a shame this body had never been granted a completely devastating lay.

And what a paltry number of test cases to draw from. The second, and last—my husband, Stuart. The first (and what a blow to hope eternal)—Charles (Chuck) Lowell, a gorgeous hunk of a W.A.S.P. from Princeton.

I stood in front of the closet-door mirror, looking through myself, seeing a reflection of the past.

It is thirteen years and two centimeters of uplift ago. I wear my hair in a long ponytail and am learning how to put a little English on my serve. I am living in a cubicle in Main Dormitory. It is my senior year. I am majoring in Philosophy and minoring in masturbation. I have an occasional hot date but never let it go further than fumbling and fingering. One day a corridor mate introduces me to her brother, Charles, an American history major whose perfection is his only flaw. He thinks I am pretty and "interesting" and invites me to a weekend at Princeton, where we engage, after a football game, in heavy petting in one of the nooks of Terrace Club. He discovers that I am, genitally speaking, a tight-lipped tease and accepts the challenge with zeal. I feel the old moral fiber weakening.

The *coup d'etwat* takes place in my cubicle one balmy spring Saturday when I am feeling especially free (I've done all my Monday assignments) and especially fulfilled (I'm taking a painting course and I'm finally beginning to achieve that warm glow of competence). I just know that this is going to be the afternoon. I've got *Carmina Burana* playing on my phonograph, blocking out sounds of campus life. I am lying on my Indian print bedspread with all my clothing opened, raised, unzipped, and unhooked. The Princeton god, shirtless and gleaming, is laying open-mouthed kisses down my throat and gently rolling my nipples between his fingers. The door is locked. (If anybody wants to borrow class notes, or a book, or my red cashmere sweater, please piss off.) Soon one of his hands lovingly glides down my body towards my underpants, slips inside, and begins to fondle the hothouse flower.

It is going to happen today. I can feel it coming. This is it. I am going to experience the rupturous raptures of what-it's-all-about. A glorious, smooth penis is actually going to be inserted up into my glorious, smooth territory unchartered, and I am going to be filled with beautiful explosives! Poetry!

My pants are off now. My legs are hanging open. Chuck is standing naked by the bed, getting something from the pocket of his pants. His penis is reaching out a mile. He takes a condom out of his pocket (How many does he have? Do they come separately or in economy packs?) and deftly slips it on, like a surgeon's glove.

Will it be painless? He lies on top of me. He kisses me. He grinds against me. He rises, takes hold of his organ and very deliberately guides it into my vagina. Up. Up. Up. There is a stretching sensation, initial discomfort, no real pain. I'm doing it. I am really doing it. Look ma, I'm—Oh, Jesus, don't look, ma. Pump and bump. Pump and bump. Pump and bump.

Pump and bump. Pump and bump. But what is happening here? Why have I not begun to gyrate uncontrollably? Why am I not moaning—doesn't everybody moan? This thing in me feels more like a super tampon than an ecstasy-bearing rod. I'm waiting, I'm waiting. This is a goddamn responsibility! He's pushing

7

and hanging on until I can come too, but he hasn't got all day and I'm thinking that's what it might take, as the phonograph needle goes click, and the arm lifts off at the end of the record. Relax. Relax to the hum of the transformer. Hummmmmmmmm. Hummmmmmmmm. (I hear campus sounds riding the breeze, drifting in through the open window—girls calling to each other across bikes. Are they pedalling to the library to study? To Skinner to practice the piano? To the Juliet, just outside the gates, to see a revival of *City Lights*? Am I the only one being laid around here?) Relax. Hummmmmmmmm. Hummmmmmmmm.

Am I frigid? Oh no! I really start rotating in earnest, striving and writhing up against Chuck (he's already fired off and is hanging in there with all-American grit), trying to get my clitoris to wire a message down the tube. I start picturing Chuck doing all sorts of things to me, upside down and sideways. Then to others. Then I am helping him with the others. Thighs are spread wide, vaginal lips are pried open, tongues are exploring around and into rosy avenues. Now mouths are sharing turns around Chuck's organ, saliva is dripping down onto the balls, arched backs spread and flatten white breasts, dark organs are stroking the white breasts. Here I come. It's building up, coming to a peak, as Chuck is pressing his wilted organ against me. What the hell, I don't really have to, but I moan. It is coming, coming. Aaaah. A little flurry of tiny muscles blip, blip, blip, blipping, and it is all over.

During future love-making with Chuck, the sheer novelty is no longer as much of a distraction, and I am able to reach my fluttery orgasms a hair's breadth more quickly. But I am finally bird dogged at a Vassar dance by a female version of the West Point plebe—tall, blond, and super-secure. They are meant for each other, as by this time I know we aren't, but it hurts all the same. Deep down I still feel that rapture is possible, but I worry about my theory never gaining empirical proof. My grades rise to 3.9 as compensation.

I sank into the oily liquid of my tub. The soothing water caressed my body and a romantic feeling of expectancy washed over me. My pores opened and my mind closed to the blue tiles and the stockings drying overhead and the lines in my husband's face as he is about to formalize an act of love.

I swirled the water around my breasts and replaced all specificity with the unclear image of my true love, whoever he was.

Married and nonadulterous for twelve years, I still hadn't entirely given up my prepubescent fantasy of my knight in shining armor. He had taken on a few son-of-a-bitch qualities since my childhood, but the fact that his soul complemented mine to perfection had remained the same. He had aged, too, of course. The tender flush of seventeen had been replaced by a weathered, ruddy look, and the innocent smile had become rakish. But he was still dark and lean and his breath still caught at the sight of me. He had waited for me to mature, and then his sex mania (held in check for so long) had become a sweet gift to me alone. In my dreams he ravished me gently and often.

Was this perfect mate the lost half-self with whom I was once combined to form a perfect whole, as the Platonic story goes? Was he the end of some teleologic plan? Or was he simply the result of a routine screw? I was concerned only with his existence, upon which I was counting, and his arrival in my world. Where was he at this very instant? In Cleveland reading Thomas Mann? In Brazil scratching his crotch?

I spread my legs, and felt the delicate pressure of the water between them.

It is a setting made hectic by noisy traffic or dancing couples. Our eyes meet and after a brief exchange of witty and biting sarcasm, which serves to relieve the intensity of the attraction and also to make its consummation more delicious, we exit together arm in arm and are forevermore entwined in a relationship which continuously renews itself. The wedding ceremony is brief, but touching. I cry. He is quietly eager. The children are well behaved, and my husband—who becomes my ex- by instantaneous decree—looks on in awe at what he recognizes to be a miraculous union. Prurience and purity forming a life style greater than the sum of its parts.

I created an eddy with my right knee, sending a small current of sweet-smelling bath water between my thighs. I was becoming a receptive instrument of love as I relaxed further and let my legs open wider. My hand—*his* hand—rose to my breasts and stroked them until my nipples became taut and my heart beat more rapidly. I threw back my head as I (he) continued to manipulate my breasts, rubbing the nipples with his palm until they tingled. His hand roamed over my breasts and belly, slippery smooth from the bath gel, pressing and fondling until I could bear it no longer. I ached in that hungry mouth between my legs, where I craved motion and pressure. He finally let his hand slip along my belly to stroke the tender lips. He knew just when it was time to part the labia, and massage the cushioned passage to my imploring center. I writhed and pressed up against his kneading fingers as they knowingly made the transition from tenderness to firmness. I arched toward him until the yielding pulsations of my climax were reached. And sought and reached again, more quickly.

Lying in the tub afterwards, my face still throbbing, my body not quite sated by my solipsistic love-making, I gazed at the blue tiles and wondered if I should feel misgivings.

Because I considered myself to be merely unfulfilled, not narcissistic, and because I no longer permitted myself to engage, more than rarely, in such orgasmic flights of fancy (a technique, I should remember, at last acquiring status!), I decided that any regrets were inappropriate.

And to prove my point I engaged in one more lively round of self-gratification before getting dressed.

2

Harrison's Real Estate Agency was just off Main Street in Hampton Village. I got there at 1:30 and paused to glance in the window at the local houses for sale. They ranged from a little cottage in Speonk, taken close-up to eliminate surroundings, with crisp tie-back curtains hanging in the window (wasn't it quaint to be lower middle class?) to a palatial residence in Quogue, surrounded by smooth lawn and royal trees trimmed with patience and pride (wasn't it grand to be rich?). Real estate photographs always made me feel sad. Those Woolworth-framed properties with their fenced in rose gardens seemed to show how narrow dreams become. Faded from the sun, they reminded me of worn linoleum and friends I never wrote to anymore.

Miss Gloria Connolly, Harrison's gal friday, saw me through the glass and waved to me as I came in.

"Hi, Mrs. Hiller. How're you doing?"

"Fine. You?"

Gloria smiled. Her frosted peach lipstick matched her dress. "Not bad."

I sat at Mr. Harrison's oak desk and dropped my bag on the floor. "Any messages for me?"

"Yes. Mr. Harrison says come in Thursday. Some people are coming in from the City for summer rentals." ("The City," as if there were only One, referred to Manhattan. Looked upon with ambivalence by eastern Long Islanders, it was that metropolitan savant that thrilled your sensibilities while stealing your gold chain.)

"Got their names and numbers?"

"Here it is." I took the paper from her. The names and pertinent notes were scribbled in Mr. Harrison's barely legible script:

11:30 Mr. and Mrs. William Bantom 678-7680 off: 546-0032 show
  NR-1,2,4—call Tully's first
12:30 Gil Ramsey off: 579-9910 ext 701—G-5etc.
 1:30 Donald McGuinness and Matthew Devon 417-3876 (h&off)
  NRs
 2:30 Dr. and Mrs. Leonard Weinstein off: 338-9953 (24 hr serv)
  NR-1, M-2,3,5 discourage HCntry Clb

"I guess the Club has already filled its quota," I said curtly. Having been conceived by a Jewish naturalist and a Catholic indecisive, I learned about justice from birth. My parents' first tenet: Be tolerant, open-minded, and liberated in thought. Their second: Keep your cunt under lock and key. The first, we conversed freely about. The second was never explicitly stated, but learned through oblique references and shy evasions. My parents are Moral and Metaphysical sophisticates; gut-ethic infants. "I understand. Do you want me to cover the telephone while you go out for awhile?"

"No thanks," replied Gloria, her eyes averted as she looked for a piece of lint to brush from her dress. "I've got some letters to type."

"See you Thursday, then." I glanced at all the house keys on the rear wall. They were hanging near one of the south fork's original-oil-dune-scenes—flat expanse of sand, lone gull perched on broken fence; cool, smooth and mass-producible. I should start painting again. I was better than that, damn it.

Even as I crossed the threshold of the office, I was estimating time. Time to go to the bank? Check. Time to run to Gristede's? Check. Time to go to the post office? Check. Time to tell Bill's meat to take a flying fuck? Check.

In Gristede's I bumped into Sue taking a break from Bobby, whom she had left with a sitter. She seemed a bit jumpy, and I wasn't sure whether it was due to Bobby's illness or recovery. She kept shifting her weight, looking around as if she were being followed. "You were in a crazy mood when I spoke to you on the phone," she said, distractedly running her fingers through her hair. (I loved her hair. It was dark blond, smooth, and straight. Parted in the middle, it formed a fine outline for her delicate features, which needed no more than that. Susan considered it drab and limp. She valued none of her attributes. She was a lithesome 5 feet 11 inches and hated herself for it. The kids on her block used to call her a string bean and she must have begun cringing then. Her husband, a stocky 5 feet 8 inches, did nothing to repair her self-image. In fact, he sometimes teased her about her proportions.)

"How's Bobby?"

"All right, I guess. He ran into a lamp this morning and broke it. Roger will be furious."

"Come on, he'll understand."

Will he? Roger's pleasantness seemed studied, a thin veneer over a surly nature. His smiles were too fleeting; his body language introverted, except on the tennis court. Stuart and I always had our most active disagreements when we mutually and ineffectively tried to compensate for his bullish net game. I didn't know him very well, but in the everyday game of human encounters I thought he might very well be a passive aggressive—a cloaked bastard.

Focusing on a spot somewhere near my left foot, Susan stiffened, and, in a pitch above normal, asked me if I could drop over for coffee the next morning.

"Want to talk now?" I asked, concerned.

"No."

I left Susan at the check-out counter and drove to the bank to transfer mortgage money from the savings to the checking account (life must go on and bills get paid even while friends suffer and one's cunt aches).

It was raining when I emerged, disconcerted, from the meat market. Although I found it exhilarating to challenge an offender, I became embarrassed when he retaliated with apologies and a fresh piece of meat.

By the time I picked up the mail at the post office it was pouring. I drove to the bus stop so John and Laura wouldn't have to walk the long block home, unprepared for rain. It was a little early. I sat in the car, looking through the mail, feeling that gnawing disquietude that had become chronic. Lack of definition. Sexual discouragement. The feeling that I was consuming time, not mind—that my life was becoming an absurd waiting game. That I was not demanding enough of myself. That I should be painting. Shut up, I will do something about it.

I pulled out *The New York Review of Books* from the pile of mail and turned to the classified ads. Business Opportunities. A calligrapher needed in New Haven. A writer of "short, simple" articles wanted in Omaha. Tough luck. How about the Personals. Maybe I'd apply for something here. Here was a good one.

EMOTIONALLY MATURE, WARM, HANDSOME WRITER, male, 38, seeks attractive female 25–35, educated, affectionate, vulnerable, nonsmoker, who desires dynamic relationship to fulfill compatible fantasies. NYC area. NYR, Box 15648.

Now, how would I go about reporting to this charmer?

Thirty four and looking for Mr. Right to carry me away to dreams beyond reality. Will settle for multiple orgasms with HANDSOME WRITER of 38. Vulnerable, as required. Nonsmoker with pearly teeth. Inactive painter with poor excuses. Educated? Will forward old term paper so you can see what I could once do. Dark green eyes, delicate nose, sensuous mouth, in oval setting. Framed by thick, shiny,

14

dark brown hair, bluntly cut just above shoulders. Body economical but shapely. Narrow waist leading to round, compact ass. Nicely tapered thighs and calves, youthful, tennis-tough. Flat belly bearing a few practically undetectable rays of stretch marks acquired during pregnancy (what do you want, perfection, for Chrissake?). Breasts, a couple of perky handfuls. All in all, quite fuckable. Hoping to hear from you soon. NYR, Box 6900.

I sat musing and moping in the car until I caught sight, in the rear view mirror, of the school bus making its way to my street. No matter what my state of mind, I always had that same feeling of love-sweet excitement when, out of the children jumping and tripping off the bus, I spotted the two whose every crease and crevice I knew. Among the occasions when my feelings were pure and absolute were when I saw them sleeping, holding hands, blowing out birthday candles, and getting off the school bus.

Laura and John pounced into the back of the car. Laura leaned forward for a kiss and I kissed her nose. "Hi, sweets. Look at all those papers!"

"It's the lunch menu and my pictures. John get off. You're sitting on my coat!"

"How was the math test, honey bun? And get off Laura's coat," I said to John, who was teasing Laura with a smile.

"We don't get our marks back until tomorrow. I think I got two wrong."

Don't say it, I thought. Hold yourself back. He'll get into college. He'll be a success. Don't! "How come?" I asked. There, I couldn't help myself!

"I don't know," said John, giving his sister a gratuitous kick. "If I knew how come, I woulda got 'em right."

Touché. Maybe if he didn't go to college he could write situation comedies for NBC. "Would have gotten them right," I corrected.

Poor kids. Why did I want so fiercely for them to succeed according to my standards? Too easy to explain it by means of the old parent-vicariously-fulfilling-goals-through-children gambit. Maybe they were my surrogate canvases. What an easy way out of facing the labor and possible failure of painting. It wouldn't work, though. When they were born the feeling of having been a creator was like a Bruckner fanfare, but it didn't take the place of artistic achievement for long. The baby-making skill is gratuitous. There's no act of independent thoughtful production or self-creation to it. Now that the birth rites no longer filled that need, was I trying to mold the helpless things to fit my specifications? Were they art projects of mine? Was there a danger of my going beyond guidance to exploitation? Back off!

Laura cried to John, "Don't kick me, you bastard!" as we drove down the wet street.

"Laura!" I shouted. How labile I was. Within minutes I had hit peaks of love, guilt, and hostility. "Don't talk like that. Do you hear me?" Back to the petty, predictable wearing away of time.

"I'm sorry," said Laura.

Irritation mounted as we ran from the car to the house, and Laura accidentally dropped her favorite picture (or what *became* her favorite picture as it dropped) into a puddle.

Gathering strength, I strode to the back room where I kept the bank books, bills, and other memorabilia. I posted Mr. Harrison's paper on my bulletin board—filled with timely notices and obsolete plans, like the Russian circus that had long ago come to and gone from the Nassau Coliseum—and posted the deposit in the bank book.

The phone rang on schedule. Stuart would be home at 5:45, his secretary informed me officially.

So what else was new?

I sat on the edge of my side of the bed and wondered if it were worthwhile inserting the arcing spring diaphragm, which I kept in my underwear drawer. Stuart's sexual needs generally waned during the tax season and he probably would not be requiring ejaculation tonight. However, it was very inconvenient to jump up and grope for the device should the need (or Stuart's organ) arise during the night. Having to stop and shove a springy rubber object up one's orifice was also detrimental to sustaining a simulated romance, and I decided to be prepared, after all. I isolated my ovum.

As I removed the brown and white Bill Blass bedspread—bought not long ago on sale at Bloomingdale's—I noted, once again, that the spread did not seem to suit the twelve-year-old pine furniture. But what did it matter, anyway? The bedroom itself, like its occupants, seemed to be a composite of incohesive elements and inadequate compromises. Even the serene Andrew Wyeth reproduction (his purchase) seemed to be at odds with the expressionistic original (my endeavor) hanging on an opposing wall. (Remember? I painted this one just before I met Stuart. I was just out of college—working in the art department of an ad agency and taking classes at the Art Students League a few evenings a week. I was living at home, under the illusion that I was free. Stuart, four years my senior, was the son of friends of my parents. Our meeting was the by-product of a small dinner party—an a priori celebration, I suspect, of our meeting.

Remember? How I liked being out with him when we were dating, he was so handsome and tall. How, as a young C.P.A., he was tactful, tasteful, and sensible, and finally convinced me that our marriage would be a sound one. Like one of his accounts? How I tried to overcome the intuitive feeling that our tidy little knot would come undone. How, with a little prodding from my mother and a few doubts about the maturity of my doubts, I put my fantasies in reserve and hoped that I could strive my way to fulfillment and earth-moving lays with him.)

I lifted my long yellow nightgown and slipped under the covers. I was about to pick up an Agatha Christie but at that moment Stuart emerged from the shower, all scrubbed and rosy, modestly wrapped in a towel, saronglike.

He was so good looking—thick wavy brown hair, neatly trimmed, dark brown eyes which one might easily interpret as penetrating, clean classic features. A bug on physical fitness (my most appreciated gift was a Hoffritz pedometer to take along on his scheduled jogs), he was also lean and muscular. Damn it, why did I find him so bland!

"Did you flush the toilet while I was showering?" he asked. "The pressure suddenly went kaput."

"No," I answered, turning off the light as Stuart delicately removed his sarong and got into bed close to me. In spite of it being the tax season, I could tell he was going to request some form of internal revenue from me tonight.

"How did John's math test go?" he asked. "I forgot to ask him."

"He got two wrong."

"Not bad."

"Out of six?"

"Oh."

I thought I had better start getting ready for our sexual encounter or I'd be dry as a bone when Stuart was ready to go, and I handled that situation awkwardly, never knowing what to say to him, he seemed to embarrass so easily. I started working on the exercises my gynecologist said were good for building muscle tone after two pregnancies. (Dr. Blau had inserted a finger into my vagina and told me to grab onto it. "Very good," he praised, as his nurse looked on.) I had discovered that it was also a good exercise for getting the juices going and creating a context of sexual urgency.

"John's a smart boy," Stuart mused. "He'll be all right." He turned on his side towards me and felt my right breast as if he were looking for nodules.

I continued contracting and releasing the muscles in my vaginal wall, and as Stuart continued his medical examination, I could feel myself becoming moist and ready.

Stuart lifted up my nightgown under the cover and, without so much as a preparatory caressing of a thigh, zeroed in on the spot well behind the clitoris, which he proceeded to manipulate with mechanical vigor. S. Hiller, C.P.A.—Certified Pubic Attendant. He was a smart man who could add three columns of figures at once. Why couldn't he remember where to massage me?

On several occasions I had indicated, by pushing his fingers to the location, where I wanted to be touched the most at the beginning, but he either hadn't understood my meaning, or had

18

failed to retain it. If we could only *verbalize* our feelings! But how do you talk to a man who, after twelve years of marriage, still ran the water in the sink every morning to disguise the sound of his peeing? How do you refer to your clitoris, or to the pressure with which you want it touched? How do you refer to the organ suspended between his legs so he may be able to direct its activity to your mutual satisfaction? Can you actually say "penis" out loud? How about "stout member" or "turgid protuberance" or just plain "thing"? Could you say "Put IT in gently, don't ram IT down," to a man who has never been able to accept a kiss on his you-know-what without noticeably flinching, and still has not been able to bring himself to kissing yours? (He had gotten as far as lightly brushing my labia majora once, and backed off in veiled disgust, and I hadn't been able to bring myself to say, "Hey! That feels good. Where are you going?") He made a pretense of caring that my desires were fulfilled, but that was because he wanted me to be a happy receptor. He had a strong regard for propriety, balance, directness, custom, and cleanliness. In other words, he was a short-order cock. Deep, *deep* down maybe he craved to suck, gnaw, lick, and devour, but with my history and his genteelness, we weren't about to find out. I needed a little more encouragement or chemistry. I could flippantly use pornographic language when joking around, but when engaged in a serious fuck with my husband, I lost my nerve.

Stuart now prepared to enter me. Hurriedly he mounted, parted the gates (Be gentle! I called from inside my head), and plunged. (Ouch! He had not received the subvocal communication.)

We kissed, tentatively open-mouthed, feigning abandonment. He reached under me and held my buttocks in a grip like a vise, and began his rhythmical journey towards climax. I clasped him around his shoulders and embraced his torso with my legs. And together, but separately, with our own private visions and abstractions we reached our orgasms. Like strangers on the same train, we arrived together at the station, without ever meeting.

"I feel very good. Do you?" Stuart asked afterwards.

19

"Yes," I exaggerated.

We had at last spoken, if only obliquely, on the subject of fornication.

3

Rain or shine, menstruating or not, Susan and I were scheduled to play doubles at the Hampton Tennis every Tuesday and Friday from eleven to one. With six other females, ranging in aptitude from a modest "A" to a pushy "B—," we vied on the clay courts and showed our true colors. Basic personalities emerged, could almost be diagrammed, as physical exuberance and competitiveness operated within the framework of rules and white lines, and freedom and restraint came to grips within each of us.

The elements of society were crystallized from eleven to one on Tuesdays and Fridays, and analogies were inevitable. Susan, for example, was cautious at the net and rarely took high-risk shots, characteristically denying her height as an asset. She was apologetic when she made an error and rarely poached.

Nancy bent over backwards in judging opponents' balls as "just catching the tape." She had Dri-grip for everybody and was forever yelling "Good shot!" to one and all, hoping she would be loved.

Gladys smiled a lot, but had been known to mutter "Fuck!" when her partner missed a shot. She shouted "Mine!" regarding a ball which was obviously "Yours," and smashed at lobs sailing out of the court.

I'd hit a shallow second serve rather than double fault, and hated myself for it. I was very aggressive in the back court and kept promising myself to rush the net, just as I wished I could rush at life and be less fearful of the consequences.

On Tuesday morning at nine o'clock I dropped by Sue's house in East Quogue as promised.

Susan looked worn out. It was two days before her period, she said quickly, straightening her robe, so I figured any disorder in her life would be at its most invasive. She clicked on the coffee appliance and brushed a strand of hair away from her eyes. I looked into her pale morning face and we were sisters, our lives marked by the same cycles, infused by the same fears.

The day Syria and Egypt attacked Israel in 1973, my father and I, who shun all religious identity, became outraged *sabras*. Just as we felt linked by a common threat to all the people in the world called "Jews" either by choice or historical accident, I felt linked to all women as I watched Susan tighten the knot in her robe and, sighing, plump herself down across from me in one of her yellow vinyl chairs. Has anybody but us known the embarrassment of a bloodstain on a white dress? Can anybody but us know the peculiar displacement a medical man dubbed "post-partum depression," and what did *he* know if not through interview? Analogy is not experience. Does anybody but us fear a cervical lesion and its migrating death cells? I suppose what I wanted from my knight in shining armor was for him to inhale my particular premenstrual scent and out of the miracle of love stretch his mind and *know* my ovarian cramp.

"I hardly got any sleep," she said. "I know I look it."

"I've seen you looking better. And," I shrugged, "worse, too."

She managed a smile. She had deep circles under her eyes. Blusher would have helped her complexion. She was not yet prepared for public appearance. Morning was the great equalizer, and my heart went out to us all.

"I was up half the night dredging up old memories," she said. "I guess you hold on to things that can't change when you think the rug is about to be pulled out from under you."

"What are you talking about?"

"Roger."

"Roger?"

She looked up at me, her eyes misting. "Do you know if I don't fall asleep touching some part of his body I don't feel secure? I'm so dependent—such a fanatic about him. I'm so afraid of change."

How different sisters can be. Susan was apprehensive that her world might change, and I was so afraid mine wouldn't. "What are you worried about, anyway?" I asked.

"If anything happens to . . ." She hesitated. "You know, I threw myself at him. I had a job—my first and only—as a legal secretary. It was a great job and I didn't give it a second thought. Roger carried me off into the sunset and now here I am in the dark. I'm helpless. I don't mean about money or anything. I mean about determining what *happens* to me."

"I don't know what's wrong here, but you're not helpless."

"Oh, sure. My independence gets me through sassy conversation at a cocktail party. It's pure illusion." She looked down at her lap, as if it might offer her strength. "Roger is having another affair."

I knew Roger "looked"; I didn't know he followed through. I didn't want to distress her by over- or underplaying my surprise. "You're probably wrong," I mustered.

"He's been working on the Webster house and coming home at noon. Yesterday he called to say he couldn't come home for lunch."

Roger was a builder and had in fact done some renovations on our kitchen. Ours. Stuart's and mine. How would I feel if Stuart were unfaithful to me. I would be hurt, not desperate. Hurt only out of a sense of possessive indignation. At the moment we had an arrangement and I counted on him to provide a certain tidiness to our daily lives. Selfishly, I wanted the changing of the guards to be an orderly event. I didn't depend on Stuart, however, as Sue depended on Roger, for a sense of well being. "What happened yesterday?"

She blew her nose into a napkin. "While he was on the phone

23

with me I heard muffled noises in the background. He sounded very formal with me. Ellen Webster was right there with him, I know."

"Don't you think you're reading something into what probably is nothing?"

"He crept in late last night."

"Where was *Mr.* Webster?"

"Conveniently out of town."

"Did you accuse the bastard?"

"Please don't, Joan. Yes, I did."

"Well?"

"Of course he denied it, but he was touchy about everything."

The coffee was ready and Susan poured it. "Cream and sugar? You don't take sugar." She burst into tears.

Nothing like this had ever happened to me and Stuart. Never a dramatic matter to be passionately resolved in tears or bed or both. My passions were thwarted without histrionics. Mine was the inertia of marital moderation with its concomitant lack of interest in reparation or separation. I put my hand over hers, knowing it wouldn't be enough.

"It's not only that I'm hurt," she wept. "I'm so frightened that maybe this time it's serious. I can't lose him."

Although I had once hoped for greater fervency between Stuart and myself, I had never been able to invest my undying devotion—only, at one time, its semblance—in our marriage. "You're . . . lucky you feel so strongly. I'm sure he loves you."

Susan withdrew her hand and reached across the table for a chocolate chip cookie, then began absently breaking it up into little pieces. "He left before I woke up this morning. He didn't want to face me." She stood up, gathered the cookie crumbs into a small pile, swept them into the palm of her hand, and neatly disposed of them in the plastic garbage can, thus performing one of the small bits of choreography that impose order on the unknown.

"Make him talk to you tonight. Right now I think you should

24

comb your hair, put on your green tennis dress, and say 'Fuck him.'"

The front door slammed shut before Susan could react and Roger suddenly appeared in the kitchen doorway. "Fuck who, or is it whom?" he asked, smiling at me. There was a touch of scorn in the posture of his mouth.

"Fuck you, of course."

Roger didn't give me the satisfaction of a response. He strode around the table to where his disheveled wife was trying to hold her world together by realigning the salt and pepper shakers on the shelf over the sink. "I came home to have breakfast with my little girl." He bent down and embraced Susan from behind as a tear rolled down her cheek. "I missed our morning talk over coffee."

Susan contracted awkwardly, as if trying to make herself smaller. She suddenly flung her arms around him, sobbing. He stroked her shoulder, and, as I nervously shifted my weight, his hand wandered down Susan's back and came to rest on her behind. I rose from my seat.

"See you at eleven," I said, rising.

Susan turned towards me. "Stay," she whispered, her eyes urging me to go.

"I think I'll run a couple of errands," I insisted.

I tried to picture the scene that followed. I was sure that before any attempt was made to evaluate their marital status, Roger would undo Susan's pink terry cloth robe and his fly and, with the red eye of Mr. Coffee's "warmer" light looking on, would make love to her up against the kitchen table, as the sunlight danced on the yellow and white gingham Sanitas.

Later, as I drove along Dune Road to the Bubble, I saw more carpenters and repairmen than usual along the beach road, sprucing up the houses in preparation for their summer occupants. So desolate in the winter, this flat stretch of land would soon be brimming with the summer people.

The bubble would be coming down for the summer, and a whole new crowd of fair weather friends would be preempting us winter regulars. The bathrooms would be repainted for these seasonal implants accustomed to paying a lot for a little attentiveness. Bright new towels would adorn the racks, and patterned toilet paper would replace the single sheets.

The love-hate passion would surface as soon as natives witnessed the invasion. Business would boom. Homeowning transients would pollute the nights with their stereos, but they paid their taxes without populating the schools. The summer people brought color, noise, need, speed, style into our conservative county, and about this time of year I looked forward to the shock, the shake-up, the insolence, the commotion that would distract me from my loneliness.

The beach clubs, now quiet except for the occasional hammer-sound of repair, their empty pools like huge concrete graves, would soon abound with tanning bodies, resound with squeals and splashes, warnings and whistles.

At the Marlin, local mothers accompanied by visiting in-laws and little girls in pretty two-piece suits, would lie and stroll about as if they were in their own backyards, while nearby, at La Circle, mothers, dressed as though they might be cruising the Caribbean, would be sipping gin and tonics while their daughters tore about bare-bodiced.

I thought of the empty bath houses, the bare beaches and wooden decks, and of my bare kitchen table, on which rested no promises of seasonal awakenings. For upon that polished maple surface never would a burst of love or drop of semen fall. Where Stuart lived, the act of sexual entry, like the entry in an accountant's ledger, had a place appropriated for it, and that place was not amidst the flaming fall colors of my kitchen.

Playing tennis later that morning, Susan tried to seem footloose and fancy-free. It didn't quite come off. I thought that maybe this time the kiss hadn't made the hurt all better. Maybe once too often the spontaneity of their morning sex had been tainted by Roger's intention to mollify and Susan's willingness to comply.

Ironically, Stuart's and my love life was not resonant enough to support any secondary aims like the subjection of a will. No room for power plays in our meager fucks. Attaining orgasm without embarrassment was enough of a hassle for us.

I guess I couldn't have been far from wrong about Susan because she told me, as we leaned against her car door outside the bubble, that although she and Roger had indeed made love in the kitchen after I had left, she felt that there had been a lack of conviction in his protestations of love. "The fact is," she said very quietly, as if it were a revelation, "everything seems to be getting out of control. Roger is tired of his clinging wife, and who can blame him? How long can I deceive myself? I'm not living in a doll house. I'm in a dinghy and the captain may cut me from my moorings any time."

"Shake him up."

"I'm afraid of heights. I don't want to stand on any ledges or anything."

"Funny. Be a court reporter. Learn to fix a motorcycle. Make a list of your natural resources. Change your *focus*."

"I don't know where to begin."

Across the road, on the oceanside, builders were putting up the skeleton of a new house. At this early stage it was impossible to see what the style of the house would be. One of the men noticed us and raised a hand in friendly greeting.

"Just begin," I said, as much to myself as to Sue.

4

I sat with the Bantoms ("Please call us Dusty and Bill") in the Clarks' living room in Quogue, wondering why the hell Harrison hadn't asked me to air the place out.

Bill Bantom didn't take long to let me know that his father-in-law belonged to the Order of Colonial Lords of Manors in America, being a descendant of one of the patroons of New Netherland. His wife lowered her head in aristocratic humility as he alluded to her father's lecture about colonial manors given at the society's recent convention at the Statler-Hilton.

He also dropped a few names. He and Dusty numbered among their acquaintances a popular New York theater director, an historian from Fordham University who had been interviewed by Robert MacNeil, and a best-selling author.

In short, the Bantoms represented the summer elite into whose company some of the locals try to insinuate themselves by inviting them to informal lawn parties. (The alternative "in" group was the royal order of natives whose family names were borne by various lanes and streets.)

We had just ended a discussion on the ways to combat mildew

29

and the superiority of farm stand produce. It was 12:35, and I hoped that Gil Ramsey, my 12:30 appointment, was not an impatient man. Gloria, I assumed, would be entertaining him with the latest weather forecasts. If, however, Mr. Harrison were in the office, he would be hard- or soft-selling the virtues of some of his rentals. He was clever at determining which technique to use, based on the sensitivity of the client.

Dusty extended her arm across the back of the yellow and green chintz love seat, and smiled. "I'm really looking forward to this summer. We can certainly use a few months of fresh clean air."

"After we open up the doors and windows, anyway," Bill added, sniffing the odor of mildew.

"I'm sorry we took so long at Tully's," said Dusty. "One of the disadvantages of visiting a house that's occupied, I suppose."

Mrs. Tully, an adroit and wiry widow of seventy-eight, had been both loquacious and hospitable. We were treated to tea and cake, and the itinerary of Mrs. Tully's prospective summer trip to southern Europe with her sister Eleanor. It was evident from the start, to me at least, that Dusty was not interested in making Mrs. Tully's palace of precious china and old lace doilies her temporary home, even though its location was suitable, and that knowledge had made the visit seem longer than it actually had been.

The house we now sat in was the Clarks' investment, not residence, and was, therefore, vacant. "I think you'll be happy here," I said. "The pool's terrific, isn't it?"

"Lovely," agreed Dusty.

"Will there be someone resurfacing the clay court and laying the tape and taking care of the grounds?" Bill asked.

"Oh, the Clarks will take care of all that."

"Soon, I hope," said Dusty. "I'd like to start coming out on weekends."

"I'll call the Clarks and get back to you. The price we mentioned is the flat summer rental. I'm not sure what the arrangements will be for the remainder of the spring."

"No problem," Dusty chirped. "You've been adorable. A wonderful tour guide." Dusty couldn't have been more than three or four years older than I, and yet she spoke as though she were my aunt. "This house is perfect for entertaining. I hope you'll want to come and visit. We always like to have a lot of interesting people around us."

"I'd love to," I answered, gathering together my belongings and sneaking a glance at my watch.

I dropped the Bantoms off at their Mercedes 450 and parked my own car. As I entered the agency a half-hour late, I prepared myself for a justifiably irate client.

But Gil Ramsey had not yet arrived.

As I opened the door to the office, Mr. Harrison, a jowly man attempting to recapture his youth through hair transplants, was looking over some correspondence.

"Hi," I said, as he looked up.

"Why, hello, Joan. How's it going?"

I asked about Gil Ramsey.

"Gloria spoke to him. He had some conference and won't be able to make it until five. She told him you'd call him back when you got in. Hell of a nerve."

I found the message on Gloria's desk:

Joan—Please phone G. Ramsey, 212-579-9910 ext 701 before 1:30.

"Beyond the call of duty," said Harrison.

"I'll phone my sitter and see if she can help out."

Mrs. Bennett was agreeable to preparing the London broil I had left marinating on the kitchen counter.

"I probably won't be home before my husband," I said, "so can you feed everyone at six or so?"

Next, I telephoned Gil Ramsey and discovered that I had dialed the number of Columbia University. "Extension 701, please," delivered me to the Astronomy Department, where I was mellifluously told to "hold on one moment."

"Ramsey here" was the next announcement that greeted me, and the sudden resonance made me smile.

"Hi, this is Joan Hiller—Harrison's Real Estate Agency."

"Say, I'm sorry. I hope I didn't put your day out of whack."

"Well, no."

"One of my students had a kind of emergency."

I wondered what kind of emergency one could have in Astronomy.

"A personal emergency," he added, as if reading my mind.

With my free hand I started doodling a flower on a memo pad. "It's all right, Mr.—or is it Dr.—Ramsey. I'll come back here at five."

"The name's Gil. And are you sure I won't be putting you out in any way?"

I assured him that he wouldn't. "How about *you*? Maybe you'd rather make it some time next week?"

"No. I'm coming out anyway. I'm staying over at a friend's. Actually, he's the one who recommended Harrison's. Ted—and Ann—Linden? They live in Hampton Village. Know them?"

He had a voice I was finding agreeable. "No, I'm afraid not." Mr. Harrison glanced at me and I knew he was thinking about long distance rates. "I hope you don't run into much traffic on the expressway."

"Don't worry. I promise I'll be on time."

Our next clients arrived promptly at 1:30. Mr. Matthew Devon, slim and mincing, with an ass like a melon, and Mr. Donald McGuinness, erect and neat, though slightly dissipated, as evidenced by broken capillaries in a bulbous nose. I imagined him coolly penetrating Mr. Devon's perfect little sphere while reaching in front to caress his tender balls. This vision of intimacy contrasted with our less than cordial conversation. Even as we discussed the waterfront file of summer rentals, I felt excluded from their whispered asides. I tried to be cheerful and direct. I felt foolish and loud.

I drove them in my Volkswagen, stopping at several places they showed some interest in. Mr. McGuinness, the more decisive of the two, was more eager to please his companion than himself. Although they were going to another agent in town that afternoon, they seemed tentatively satisfied with a waterfront property in Hampton Village that sported a charming sun room, a modest pool, and an asphalt tennis court that was covered with a thin layer of sand. I could see them sweeping it off together, and, afterward, Mr. McGuinness losing a set to the younger Mr. Devon, the sight of whose supple body glistening in the summer sun more than making up for the defeat of tired limbs.

At 2:40 Dr. Leonard Weinstein, gynecologist, and Mrs. Weinstein, his secretary/wife, appeared at the agency. Mr. Harrison was almost *too* gracious. Mrs. Weinstein and the children were going to spend the summer. The doctor was planning on weekends when he wasn't on call. She wanted a house with all the trimmings. He would settle for "anything out of my beeper's range." She mentioned the Country Club. He shot a glance over at Mr. Harrison and made a quick diagnosis. "We'll look into it, dear." I smiled slyly at him and he smiled back. I could see he didn't give a damn. I liked him. I took them around to a few houses and they were going to mull things over. If any new offerings arose, I would call them.

At 4:15 Gloria retired to the bathroom to freshen her make-up and comb her hair. Mr. Harrison left for the day, carrying a portfolio of letters, leases, and deeds to look over in the comfort of home. I called the Clarks to inquire about rental arrangements for the Bantoms, and was told by Mrs. Clark that she was amenable to early occupancy.

Gloria, her lipstick freshly applied, emerged from the bathroom and checked the contents of her wallet. "You'll lock up?" she asked as she prepared to leave for the day.

"Yes. Have a nice evening."

Alone, I called home and spoke to Mrs. Bennett, who assured me that the household was intact. John got on to complain of Laura's unwillingness to get out of his room while he was doing his homework, then Laura got on to state that John wouldn't leave her alone.

33

The door opened just as I was ending my conversation with Laura. As I was saying "Goodbye and be good, snooks," a man walked into the office, and the chemical aggregate called woman perceived, with as much insistence as a heartbeat, its means to a perfect equation.

On previous romance-tinged encounters with strangers, the voice of reason had always been right there on the scene with a few words: Don't be a schmuck, it whispered, as I looked into the sad brown eyes of an Al Pacino look-alike on the 7:03 out of Hampton Village one morning and fantasized a clandestine release of passion culminating in happy tears at the Essex House. You're an infantile cunt, it grumbled, as I answered the gaze of a handsome young paraplegic, wheeling about in Sears one Saturday, with whom I imagined a lifetime of open-mouthed kisses of largess and gratitude.

Al Pacino was forgotten the moment he deboarded at Massapequa, and the bubble burst for the handsome young paraplegic when I caught sight of a Flash Gordon comic book sticking out of his pocket.

But now I was gripped by an imperative feeling encompassing all the contours of my life, from the titillation of my clitoris to the well-being of my soul, and the voice of reason could only sing its hosanna.

I replaced the telephone receiver in its cradle and when I offered my hand, he offered his. His hand was large and warm and he paused almost imperceptibly before withdrawing it. "I'm Gil."

"I'm Joan. You're a little early. Have a seat." I blushed.

He ran his hand through his thick, chestnut brown hair. Then, smiling hesitantly, sank his tall figure opposite me into the leather chair. "The trip took less time than I thought it would." The smile lit up his strong features with a boyish charm. A tiny chip in a front tooth made it irresistible.

"Less time? Oh," I said. "I thought you would run into traffic." I guessed his age to be about thirty-two.

"Well, no. I didn't. Not much, anyway."

"Oh." My talent for witty banter, once so lively on blind dates, was in a state of paralysis.

Gil moved his long leg and the muscle of his thigh was outlined beneath his gray flannel slacks. I could see the angle of his patella, pressed against the gray fabric.

"It looks like it might rain," he said.

"Does it?" I asked, picturing myself huddled beneath his raincoat.

"Yes, it does." Our looks met in sweet embarrassment. He adjusted the wire-rimmed glasses that had not shielded me from the penetrating dark brown eyes.

Sitting opposite Gil, my old fantasy lover became obsolete, like a charge card from a store that had gone out of business. I looked down at my hands folded on the desk, and wished that I hadn't picked my cuticles. "Well. Let's see what we have for you in the way of a summer retreat."

Gil sat back and placed his hands on his parted knees. He smiled nervously, every gesture conveying a self-conscious, vulnerable sensuality to me.

"I'll get the information." (I will have to stand up now, and get the folder from the file cabinet. He will evaluate my body and notice my damp skirt.) I casually raised myself and, passing my hand along my rear as if to smooth the wrinkles in my skirt, I checked to see if the juices of my impertinent mucosa had gotten past my nylon panties. No, thank god. I got the folder that might be appropriate for him, and sat down.

"I think we'll find something here." I smiled. (Was I feeling a little braver?)

He cleared his throat. "I hope so."

I glanced down at the folder, trying to focus my attention on rentals and away from the supplication coming from the furrow between my legs. "How large a family must the cottage accommodate?" (How cagey.)

"Just me. I'm really looking for a very modest place where I can work. I can't afford oceanfront. Walking distance would be nice, but it's not essential. I'd like to take a walk along the beach before breakfast."

(I'll get up at five in the morning. We'll walk together and you'll kiss my toe where it was cut by a shell, and then I'll make fried eggs and English muffins.) "What kind of work are you doing? Or am I being too nosy?"

"I'm writing a book on solar physics and I want to finish the final draft before the fall semester."

(After eggs and muffins, I'll type for you and make suggestions about sentence structure.) "Solar physics is one of the gaps in my education," I said, riffling through the contents of the folder.

As we talked about the apartments and cottages available in his price range, and the stores, restaurants, and other facilities in town, I became accustomed to the importunings of my vulva and found it easier to adapt myself to the business of the day.

But when he sat next to me in the car and I could smell his wild hair and see the small scar on the side of his neck and the freckle on his ear lobe, I had to struggle again to rise above the entreaties of my body.

And when I fumbled with the key to a little white cottage in Hampton Village and he took it from me, our fingers touched and my lips parted instinctively.

Changes in weather, textbooks, hair styles, movie marquees, and official attitudes regarding the easy fuck are delayed in their journey out to eastern Suffolk. Which may help to explain my awkwardness when Gil, accepting the overtures of my parted lips, bent to kiss them, tentatively, barely making an impression on the film of cherry lip gloss, as he unlocked the door.

"I'm sorry," he apologized, seeing my look of bewilderment. "I thought you . . . I don't usually . . . oh, let's go in."

I looked up at his uneasy smile. Damn, what made the sensation so exquisite? What happened back there in the office? Did the simple choreography of his opening the door just *so,* happen to strike some deep primal accord?

Not knowing what to say, I at least tried to smile knowingly, as

I walked past him into the cottage. I began making a survey of its interior with a determination that must have belied itself. First concentrating on the main room, which served as a living-dining-cooking-center, I checked the stove, sink, refrigerator, ceiling, walls, and seating arrangement.

Gil, having followed me in and closed the door, stood in the middle of the room, looking confused.

I peered into the tiny bedroom, cheerfully papered in red and yellow tulips, and tried to avoid the feelings aroused by the double bed, too large for the room, whose nubby white spread concealed who knew what pleasures of summers past.

I turned from the room and, focusing just past Gil's shoulders on a neutral vase containing dried leaves, I asked him if he liked the cottage.

"I think so," he said, as he, too, began the obligatory tour.

Afterwards we stood in the main room like two clods waiting for a cue from the prompter. "It would be nicer if it were closer to the ocean," I said.

"Well, it seems good enough. It doesn't cost much more than I can afford. Five years of summer courses ought to cover it. I like it."

Avoiding the dangers of the wicker love seat, I sat down in one of the matching chairs, padded with cushions of blue and white ticking. Gil sat down in the wicker chair opposite. "Is this when I sign on the dotted line?"

"Don't you want to see a few more places?"

"I made up my mind."

"It's as if you make decisions like this every day."

"No. This is a new experience." He looked down at his hands.

My breasts were straining against the confines of my bra. My face was flushed. The pathway between my legs yearned to be trafficked, and my hands, to reach out and touch. "Harrison can have the lease ready in a week, I think."

"Good. And the deposit?"

"A small one."

"I'll write out a check when we get back to the office, all right?"

"Yes."

Neither Gil nor I made a move to go.

Suddenly Gil placed the key to the cottage on the glass-topped coffee table that separated us. "Do you have any children?" he asked, unexpectedly, looking at the wedding band encircling my finger.

"A boy and a girl."

"And your husband? Is he in the real estate business?"

"He's an accountant—in Riverhead." I thought of Stuart in his leather and chrome office, giving instructions to the crisp Miss Larkins, unaware that at this very moment I was relinquishing my soul to a stranger.

"You haven't always lived out here—or have you?" Gil asked.

"No. We moved here from Manhattan about eight years ago when Stuart—my husband—became a partner of one of the C.P.A.'s who practiced in Riverhead. It was a good business opportunity. His partner died a few years ago. He's alone now."

"Do you like living all the way out here?"

"I could be happier." (Teasing bitch.) "How about you?"

"I don't care for the triple locks, but I wouldn't want to be in Ted's shoes either."

"Ted. The friend you're staying with."

"Right. He's teaching marine bio out at Southampton College."

"A little like retiring early, I guess?"

"Yeah, but he's a lazy Cousteau at heart."

"And you're the diligent Copernicus?" I had a vision of a creamy act of intercourse under the changing constellations of the Hayden Planetarium. I was looking straight up into the jeweled darkness, my hair pressed against the headrest, my ass on the edge of the seat, as he knelt before me, pushing his organ between my legs, his face into my neck.

He smiled. "Well, I work hard, anyway."

The wicker love seat was becoming more and more of a persuasive vacancy. "Do you come into Manhattan often?" he asked.

"About once a month. It's a shot in the arm."

"Does your—husband come in too?"

"He doesn't like the commotion."

"I have a couple of tickets for the Hollander recital at Alice Tully next Saturday. Do you think you might want to come?" He shifted his weight and looked away. Too late, the invitation was out. "I—uh—bought an extra ticket for my sister who was supposed to be coming in next week, but can't make it. He's playing Copland and Brahms."

(Who the hell cares what he's playing!) "It sounds great. I'd love to come."

He turned back. "Do you want to meet for dinner?"

For dinner? And—oh! Up to then I was only a latent sinner. At that moment I saw myself careening towards a real live illicit screwing. And Stuart? Unsuspecting, guiltless and, as his mother would say if god forbid she knew—"He *meant* well!" The little Bar Mitzvah boy, buried deep in the heart of my sophisticated father, was once again transmitting his ethic, along with that of the little Catholic cherub who fidgeted in the recesses of my mother's memory. But, challenging all codes and qualms, I mustered my courage and answered bravely:

"Okay."

"I'll call you during the week. When will you be in the office?"

"I'm in and out. Maybe I should call you."

"I'll give you my home address and phone number."

I looked at the information he recorded in my spiral pad. What delights awaited me in apt 5B on 118th and Broadway? I put the pad in my bag and rose to leave. "I think we'd better get back to the office now."

Gill stood up slowly, his tan corduroy sports jacket falling into place over what I imagined to be his sinewy torso. He picked up the key from the coffee table as I moved towards the door.

We heard the sound of rain as we stood facing each other at the door. "You were right about the rain," I said, looking at his hand as it rose to touch my face. My cheek and ear tingled as he gently placed his hand across them, and the subtle odor of his skin melted what was left of my reserve. His hand wandered to the back of my neck, under my hair, fingers spreading, feeling my scalp. Then again over my face, fingertips brushing against my lashes.

Surprisingly, I made the next move. The smell of his warm palm was enough of a catalyst. I was lifted above my bloodless ethic, my fucking prudence, lifted and tilted away from habit and towards myself.

It was as though an animal in me that had been trapped for years suddenly smelled freedom and, springing past trainers and guards (who turned away and secretly wished it luck), lunged towards the pleasures of the wild.

What the hell. I flung my arms around his neck and almost threw him off balance. He recovered and returned my embrace, the key falling to the floor. Our mouths came together with such force that I couldn't help worrying, even with my cunt on fire, if one of my goddamn teeth had cracked. Our tongues met and hung together as I swallowed our mixed juices and inhaled deeply. His breath, smelling like grilled cheese, made me even more ravenous and I pressed still closer. Our hearts were pounding together as his hands dropped to my ass. At the same time a terrible thought entered my mind. (Should I tell him? No, not yet. Wait.)

He took hold of my buttocks and, pulling me toward him, separated the two halves as much as he could (he was hampered by my skirt), widening the crevice of desire. I could feel his cock harden against my pelvis and as I gasped for breath his tongue plunged deeper inside my mouth and his hands lifted my skirt and found their way into the leg openings of my underpants. (Tell him now. No!)

I tore myself away from him. I had to get my clothes off. Living with my prim husband (if balls could blush, Stuart's would) I was usually as modest as a young girl with new tits. But now, out of (or at last, in) character, I had to make my body available, and fast. The animal was dying to eat and be eaten.

We undressed eagerly—I was driven by an old lust finally come to fruition—and face to face. We threw our clothes in a pile on the floor and paused briefly to look at each other.

He was thin, but tendinous. The hair on his body was light

brown and densest on the lower part of his flat belly, above his lovely, glutted cock. His glasses were hanging slightly awry, which gave him a look of inexperience, adding a spark of maternal affection to the fire of passion. As we converged and tumbled to the floor, his glasses fell off. He pushed them aside.

We clung together on the nubby white rug and the hard hot kisses he planted on my neck and shoulders sent chills of delight down my arms and chest. The impact of this new presence made me half delirious—the new, rougher texture of skin, the coarser hair, the narrower dimensions, the musky, stirring odor.

Every tactile and olfactory nerve was awake and exploring, devouring every sensation. I sucked and bit his lip, his neck, his armpits, to savor him more fully. My breasts seemed to swell, seeking contact with his skin, and the soft walls of my cunt continuing up the dark slippery tunnel cried out dumbly to be grazed, mauled, pressed against.

I felt the boundary of his being so keenly, our confrontation was so dizzyingly now and real, that it became surreal, taking on the quality of a dream. Value hung on the groping, grasping movements of his hands and lips.

He lay on top of me and my legs opened wide, wider. And then I wrapped them around his back and rose to meet the bursting cock which was gaining entrance to my hungry void. (Now? Just a little more, maybe, a little more.) I moaned gratefully as that large instrument stretched the burning mouth and buried itself deep in my belly.

We were coiled around each other, pressing our way to mutual ecstasy, when suddenly, from out of the gray skies of fact and consequence, I showered him with my second surprise. I could wait no longer.

"Stop!" I cried out hoarsely. "I'm not wearing my diaphragm!"

Gil withdrew like a flash and wasted his climactic spasms right below my belly button, leaving my vagina in a state of shock and my stomach covered with glue.

What a disappointment! How unlike the lovely dirty endings I had always admired from afar, where sense never intervenes with passion, regardless of the consequences. Fuck to my self-inflicted purgatory! Who the hell ever heard of a gorgeous moment missed because of a lousy rubber trampoline?

I lay there, all soggy and limp, holding back tears of frustration. "I'm sorry."

"It's all right, all right," he whispered, pressing his mouth against my ear, tenderly pushing away the wet hair from my temples.

And then he knelt over my wilted body, applying his attentions with renewed vigor. I lay there, giving nothing, receiving everything.

He placed one of his arms under my back and my eyes closed as he began stroking my breasts with his free hand, following the movements of his hand with firm, moist kisses. As his tongue neared one of my nipples my breath caught, and as it caressed that taut nub my breathing quickened. "More. More." He sucked and lovingly bit at the nipple, and when his tongue and lips wandered over the wet globes to latch upon the other, my arms rose above my head and my pelvis began moving fitfully.

He removed his arm from under me to massage my breasts and belly—gummy from his semen—until I spread my legs as far apart as they would go and bent my knees, so that he could gaze upon my aching center. "Oh, please."

His hands pressed along my inner thighs and began caressing the wet mouth that led to the still unsated orifice where all craving had become localized. He tenderly pinched and fondled the straining clitoris and the hot, juicy vulva, arousing me to a state of madness. I felt his body bend towards that point of mute supplication. His fingers parted the lips and his open mouth met that open, yearning mouth, pressing down and sucking in with a force that made me gasp. I held his head with my hands, afraid that he might move away, but he only pressed down harder, sucking at that tingling mound of flesh, making it sting with delicate pain.

My thigh muscles began tightening and relaxing against his head in agitated rhythm, and I rotated my hips and ground

42

against him to more fully enjoy the sucking, biting, licking, kissing that sought to engage me in a frenzy of uncontrolled delight. "Don't stop," I implored.

His hands slipped under my buttocks and he held me firmly as his tongue explored my front chamber more deeply. And suddenly my back arched and my arms fell outward, and my cunt yielded in a delicious wave of pulsations. He continued to press and push and it yielded again, the thrill drawn still further up into my belly, rippling and prickling through my body.

At last I opened my eyes. My legs hung open and relaxed, their center dripping with pleasure. An open wound, salved.

Gil was bent over me, looking at my face. His lips were fuller, and shiny from his ministrations, and he rubbed them on my neck and then kissed me gently on my mouth. We embraced and, for a few moments, silently inhaled the emissions of sweat and sex.

And then slowly, as if on cue, we looked at each other, held the take, and grinned. Wickedly.

"The rain sure does funny things to you," he said.

"I just don't know what got into me."

I had written a thesis on logical positivism—153 pages, typed! I had nursed two children through a viral disease of unknown origin! Look at me! With a previous record of vaginal discretion, I have offered that smiling slit with bold immodesty to the piercing eyes, fingers, tongue, et cetera, of this naked character whose mind—where is it now?—must have explored the far reaches of the universe!

We exploded into laughter, like children. The insanity was for me a release as significant as orgasm. Never had I felt so free. The laughter, absurd and gratuitous, and as uninhibited as my expression of sex had just been, rolled out from the depths of innocence.

I slithered and squirmed under him as he tickled my neck with his lips and teeth and goaded my amoral cleft with his knee. At last he unpinned me and we stumbled to our feet. In the bathroom we wet our faces and bellies and patted each other dry with toilet

43

paper. We found the key under his underpants and his glasses under my skirt. I put the glasses on his nose. They were a little out of shape.

As we put our clothes back on, I tried to smooth and comb myself back into the world of prior commitments, curfews and London broils. Dressed, we were at a loss for words.

We left the cottage as intimate strangers, status undefined. As I opened the door, the rain and my Volkswagen further reminded me that I was still Mrs. Hiller, and I prepared myself for a storm of guilt that would drive my escaped animal back into captivity.

But my guilt was about as potent as grandma's kiss, and my tiger, having tasted freedom, licked its chops and grandma scurried back into her parlor.

Lying in bed with Stuart after the emotional tumult of the afternoon, my paradoxical nature struggled with itself. On the one hand, I was a romantic fool. On the other, a nut for logical analysis. Knowing full well that I was ready and eager for the activization of my secret passions, I wondered if I had chosen in my eagerness a somewhat arbitrary candidate.

As Stuart's hand reached into the V of my nightgown and methodically roamed over the upper portion of my body, I contemplated the situation, Talmudic style.

> *Question: If I have been ready for years, why on* this *day of all days did I meet the man most likely to make manifest my fantasy fucks?*
>
> *Answer: If this was simply a matter of wishful thinking, I would have made it happen years ago with some other innocent bystander. Therefore, the answer must be in the realm of sheer luck, a sharp eye, and synchronous vibes.*

Stuart's hand fondled my right breast with unusual vigor, like a doctor trying to bring an unresponsive patient out of a fainting fit.

Question: Why did that man of all men ideally fulfill my aesthetic objectives without conforming to my aesthetic ideals?
Answer: My needs are more intense than my aesthetics. Therefore, the man who fulfills my needs redefines, by embodiment, my idea of beauty.

Stuart's hand raised my nightgown, lunged between my legs and began emergency treatment, as though the patient were now sinking into coma.

Question: Why does my husband, who is off the mark, as usual, continue his ministrations when he can see that tonight my orifice is as responsive as a mouth shot full of novocaine?
Answer: He does not know, sweet thing in his striped pajamas, that for once I am not trying to work myself up into some kind of clinical climax.

With both hands, Stuart kneaded my thighs, belly, breasts. Then, leaning over me, he tried to suck some life into one of my nipples, and stroke some sense into the other. A sweet tickling sensation traveled down my body, dissipating in my dormant crotch. Dead end, Stu baby.

My covert happiness was marred by twinges of guilt, and a kind of sadness. Stuart, hornier than during previous tax seasons, must certainly have been confused and upset, although he would not say so. Now that I sought no gratification from him, my sympathy was unalloyed by resentment.

Question: What the hell should I do?
Answer: Lie.

"I've been feeling sick today. I think I may be coming down with something."

Stuart abruptly ceased his attempts to make me receptive and fell back onto his pillow, too polite to express exasperation. "That's too bad," he managed to expel.

I was filled with remorse. As Stuart had worked on me like a doctor, I proceeded to administer to his needs like a nurse. With kindness and dedication, I went to reach for his organ through his pajama opening. It was, however, projecting out of its permanent press window, beginning to droop from disappointment. I gently took it in hand and held it with objective tenderness.

Although it felt very much like a frog to me, I began to squeeze it as though it elicited more affection than the slippery amphibian a fellow camper had once dumped down my bathing suit. The frog perked up.

Stuart raised his pelvis slightly, as I contracted and released my grip on the engorged organ, but aside from that subtle movement, he remained still.

I rubbed it close to its root, then concentrated on its tip, then, with both hands, enveloped its entirety in a delicate caress, quickening my movements when I thought it was ready to ejaculate. As it started its throbbing release, I slowed the rhythm of my massage and caught the creamy discharge in my palms. I discreetly distributed the semen over the striped pajamas. The frog remained puffed up for a moment, then croaked.

We lay together in silence. Then Stuart turned over onto his stomach, kissed me on the cheek, and went to sleep. My hands sticky with drying ejaculate, I closed my eyes and tried to drift off.

Question: What is more absurd than the human drama?
Answer: The dishonesty of its players.

5

The anticipation of meeting Gil on Saturday infused new life into my net game as early as Tuesday. According to the schedule the group had worked out at the beginning of the season, Gladys and I were partners that day. Together we wiped out the three other teams in straight sets. I was formidable—rushing and swiping at backhand volleys I usually would have dealt with in the back court, jumping at overheads that ordinarily would have seemed unattainable, and even, throwing caution to the wind, going to hell with myself on my second serves.

Once, near the end of the game, my assertiveness backfired. Gladys and I were both covering the net, menacing our opponents. Gladys shouted "Mine!" in regard to a ball which I chose to interpret as *mine*. With a barbaric cry, I went for the ball, and slammed it into the net. The bubble was an echo chamber, so my "Shi-i-i-i-i-it" reververated throughout the place, reducing me to the size of a pea. The instructor on court number one, in the process of picking up balls with a pupil, regarded me with contempt, and Gladys glowered at me, not for my bad manners, but for missing the shot. I recovered, but not without realizing that I had a way to go before feeling at home in a risky situation.

"You really put them away today," Gladys said afterwards, as we sat around drinking diet soda in the club room.

"I was psyched up," I said, looking down at the terry cloth sweat band around my wrist and becoming, for an instant, Goolagong between points.

Nancy and Pat, youngest and newest members of the Tuesday group, consulted the clock hanging over the entrance to the bubble registering the rented seconds. Pat took a drink of her soda. "We've got to run," she said, Nancy nodding in agreement. "The kids are putting on a Sesame Street show at the nursery school."

The six of us left in the club room had been playing together for several years. We had met on the courts and our association had been based on tennis aptitude and compatible schedules. Whatever our differences, we had become a kind of sorority. Our knowledge of each other had come from our posttennis chats, which provided a good setting for airing major gripes and minor sins. Some of us had become closer, one-to-one friends, but the semi-deep therapeutic character of our Tuesday, Friday society remained the same.

We demanded nothing of each other but a little comfort and concern. Our exchange was free. There were no debts of the spirit to pay. As Gladys once put it, "What I like about you girls is that I might have to pick one of you up at the garage sometime, but I'll never have to fake an orgasm with any of you."

Gladys, a medical school dropout, pampered herself with her husband's wealth and justified her existence on the tennis court. It was essential to her mental health that she win at least ninety percent of her games. Assessing her sturdy legs as she propped them up on a chair, she addressed one of us. "How's your daughter treating you these days, Naomi? Is she still visiting or has she let you off the hook?"

Naomi, a retired librarian, was a very agile sixty-six. She was a widow living with a younger man and her daughter disapproved vehemently. They suffered the generation gap in reverse. It was Naomi, not her daughter, who had the youthful outlook on life.

48

"Oh, she's still clucking over me. Her return flight to her loving husband and kids is in two days. Any more of this brainwashing and she'll have me convinced that I'm a sinful old lady."

"I thought you were tougher than that," Gladys said.

"Guilt is an insidious weapon. It nibbles away at your confidence until one day you find yourself walking with your shoulders stooped. I'm beginning to question my—how did the little dear put it?—my 'moral grit.'"

"Sounds like a health food," I suggested.

"Guilt," Ruth said, "is the nucleus of the family. Relax and enjoy it."

Naomi laughed. "Thanks."

Adjusting her tennis shorts, Helen said, "You know, if we reserve now and each pay a twenty-five dollar deposit, we'll get a ten percent discount on our court time next year."

Helen had settled on eastern Long Island because her husband, a vet, believed it was a safe area to raise children and cure heartworm. She had become a member of a local school board and all of her Dalton aspirations for her small rural district had surfaced. After spending some time beating her head up against the walls of the little red schoolhouse, she learned to trim her expectations to suit the will of the majority. When last noted, she was campaigning to have the old gym lights replaced.

"What do you say, shall we commit ourselves? We might lose our eleven to one time slot if we don't reserve within a week. I'll give Nancy and Pat a call, but I'm quite sure they'll be agreeable."

Susan and I were the only two who hesitated. Helen turned towards me. "Joan?"

"I'm not sure."

"Why?" said Gladys. "You planning on turning professional? Don't let today's success on the courts go to your head, kid."

I smiled. "Up yours, sweetheart. No, I just don't know what my schedule will be. I want to start painting again. Maybe take some classes."

"What happened, cookie? The N.O.W. broads finally get to you? You feel unfulfilled? Have you been abused, poor dear?"

"Not abused. More like excused." I studied her knit brow. What do I say to you, Gladys? I should be making more use of the life force? I should be breaking through old boundaries and thought habits that aren't rules but only seem so? How about I just want to throw myself back into the arena. Will you buy it, or will you just keep tapping your soda can like that?

Gladys mimed the playing of a violin. "Deeda da deeda," she crooned.

"Come on. I'm not on a feminist hang-up. Men find excuses for settling into myopic visions of themselves too." How about Stuart? He goes off every day with his little black rectangle and spends the day sheltering tax dollars and feeding numerical data into a computer. He's always been one to praise the importance of what he calls gainful employment, but there must be times when he wonders if half his brain is drying up.

Gladys sighed. "Don't mind me, Joan. You know I get pissed off at myself for having quit med school. I'm just taking it out on you." She rubbed her hands together. "How do you like *that* for a nice bit of self-flagellation? I think it's downright adorable myself."

"I do too," I agreed. "And I think *you're* adorable, with or without the initials after the name. Anyway, why don't we reserve the courts and we'll all kick in a deposit. If I drop out I'll be responsible for getting a great substitute. All right?"

"Accepted," said Gladys.

Susan had not said a word. She seemed coiled into herself. "How about you, Sue?" Helen asked. "Are the same arrangements as this year acceptable to you?"

"What? Oh, okay. I suppose so."

"What does *that* mean?" Ruth asked. "Do we have yet another spirit in transit amongst us? Frankly, I think it's just great, but I'd hate to lose you two as tennis partners."

"I'm thinking about getting a job or going back to school," Susan said.

Helen shrugged her shoulders. "Oh, well, I guess we can table the idea to reserve next year's time for another week," she said.

50

"Anybody want a mint?" she added, digging into her tennis bag.

After we left the club Sue and I stopped for lunch.

"I'm glad you're thinking about making the big push," I said, as we waited for our beefburger platters in the noisy, smoke-filled Inn, a lair in Hampton Village with good food and dirty bathrooms.

Susan took a large draft of her vodka collins. Her hair was damp. Her face was flushed. She looked beautiful. "We'll see what happens."

I took a sip of my Bloody Mary and pressed the cold glass against my cheek. "Maybe Stuart knows of a job opening that sounds good. I'll ask him."

"Okay. Thanks."

"Part time, maybe? Are you thinking about going back to school?"

"I'm thinking about getting a good, long book out of the library and forgetting about the whole thing." She began rotating her wedding band. Around and around.

It struck me that Susan's relationship to life was literal. Could the ties that bound her to its plot be suspended? Was there a reserve of protoplasmic joy that might be tapped when despair or indifference threatened? Maybe by just turning up the volume of a Paul McCartney tape, or *The Rite of Spring*? By yielding to the thunderous waves or the silence of a starry night? By nailing the perfect backhand down the line? Pow! Irrational energy pushing aside the murky slop. Thought and matter, cause and effect, universe and self, almost a singularity—separated only by a chink of awareness, appreciation. The respite, the expansive moment of thanksgiving that returns you to circumstances that seem less disheartening—can she feel it? If the story line gets fucked up, will she come up fighting? I wasn't sure. I hoped.

"What a farce it is," she said.

"What?"

"Me, getting a job or whatever. It's supposed to be a way to fulfillment?"

"Yes."

51

She sighed. "In my case, it's just supposed to *look* like that. It's really just a way to get old *Roger* scared for once. That's not a commitment. That's a pose."

"You might surprise yourself and actually enjoy getting out on your own."

"Yeah, sure. Anything you say."

The waitress, rosy-cheeked, doubtless unscathed by middle years' self-appraisal, came toward our table bearing ketchup and onions. I glanced at her small high breasts, unconfined beneath her yellow tee shirt. "Try to enjoy it, Sue. You only live once."

As the waitress walked away, I picked up a thick slice of raw onion and contemplated its wicked delights. For whom in my household was I maintaining a sweet breath, anyway? I bit into its forbidden fruit.

Like life teeming beneath the surface of an apparently quiet pool, an undercurrent of excitement quivered beneath the surface banalities of every ordinary occurrence.

Tuesday, post tennis:

Hair cut. I strive for the perfection of imperfection. Mister William blow dries his blunt cut and I feel uncomfortably neat. Mr. William, who wishes he were shaping up with Sassoon or Suga, delicately wipes the Riverhead perspiration from his brow and layer-cuts a few inches, making it more bouncy and casual. I feel looser, more seductive. The petulant Mr. W. makes my scalp tingle as his fingers become Gil's.

A call to parents in Brooklyn Heights (hoping my voice is not tremulous) to find out if it is all right if I sleep over Saturday night. Of course it is all right. They are anxious to see me. Am I coming with . . . No? Just need a few hours of freedom, is that it? Oh. They understand. I wish I could confide in my father. I used to tell him almost everything. But I know that daddy would disapprove, advise me that my rendezvous might jeopardize my safe marriage, but really be offended on the grounds of simple morality. Anyway, I remember the days of school tests and accompanying anxieties. The only time I ever screwed up an important exam was when I anticipated a high mark and shot my mouth off. Better keep quiet and knock wood. As I mouth some self-conscious, daughterly reportage, thoughts of Gil are screaming in my head.

P.M. See an old Italian movie with Stuart. The Village Theatre is dank and practically empty. It waits, as are all the town enterprises, for the profitable influx of the Summer People. Mechanically dubbed voices echo monotonously through the theater as Sophia Loren's tits go bounce-bouncing through the streets of Naples and the avenues of dreams. The few cocks in the audience dance to the rhythm of those famous Neapolitan nipples, while my anonymous breasts stir with their own secret longing. Stuart savors his eyeful of Sophia and his mouthful of popcorn.

Wednesday:

Sacrifice. I help chaperone Laura's class, along with three other Chosen Mothers, on their field trip to the Long Island Game Farm in Manorville. I am stuck with Timmy, who mishandles the ducklings and Shirley, who goes berserk in the hay house and who can't find her liverwurst sandwich. I rescue the ducks, pick the hay out of Shirley's hair, and share my tuna fish with her. Laura cries because she says I gave Shirley more potato chips than I gave her, "your own daughter!" I feel defenseless when a group of ten calves attack me and the bottle of milk I have purchased for what I thought would be a rewarding, pastoral experience. By the time the class assembles at the animal theater to watch the ball-catching seals and the chicken that can count up to three, I am covered with dirt and I have an overwhelming desire to pee. I wait, with Timmy, on a long line for cotton candy, and then with Laura and Sally on a longer line to pee. The crescendo of desire and anticipation for my own unchaperoned adventure carries me through the noisy bus ride back to school, and I

53

even find myself singing, with some degree of enthusiasm, "We're Here Because We're Here Because We're Here" as the bus sputters into the parking lot.

Bathe myself and Laura. Then prepare to drive my children to their piano lessons—the last ones before the recital to take place at four o'clock that Sunday afternoon. John practices "On Yonder Rock Reclining" once more before his lesson, and once more throws a small suicidal fit when he forgets John Thompson's warning to "Always Be Careful to pass the thumb under smoothly." Laura responds to her brother's frustration with a snide smile and a facile rendering of Diller-Quaile's "Up in the Sky." I react with abnormally passive acceptance of my children's rotten behavior. I am distracted by the music of the spheres.

Call Susan to find out if she has started to look for a job. Roger answers the phone and seems cool, distant. It takes a few minutes for Susan to come to the phone. She says she has been tied up all day with household odds and ends, but will begin her pursuit in earnest tomorrow. She sounds weary, slow. Is it honest fatigue, or withdrawal?

Corollary. Stuart is watching television. During a commercial I tell him that Susan is looking for a job and ask him if he knows of any possibilities among his business colleagues or contacts. He asks me what Susan is "equipped" to do and I tell him "anything that requires common sense and/or secretarial skills, preferably legal." Stuart says he will "keep his ears open." At that moment I suffer a sudden and irrelevant genital disturbance to which I respond with a supreme act of sublimation, i.e., I become absorbed in the second half of a televised documentary on smog. I sit curled up in a corner of the couch, my right heel purposely and painfully digging into my crotch. This is easier to bear than the diffuse pain of agitated longing.

Thursday:

Call Gil to set up appointment for Saturday. The words are sunny and platonic, but the heart is throbbing. We plan to meet near the flowers on the main floor of the Metropolitan Museum of Art at three o'clock. A future of exquisite possibility slices through the immediate vision of a thawing brisket, the juice of which is forming a little puddle on the Formica countertop.

Go to Harrison's and follow up on a few old clients and see a few new ones:

a) After speaking with Mrs. Clark, I call the Bantoms and inform Dusty of the additional rent for the Clarks' place. Dusty accepts without hesitation, and again hopes that I and my husband ("or whoever") will be able to come to one of her tennis ("or whatever") parties.

b) Return a call to the cool Mr. McGuinness who, with the succulent Mr. Devon, has decided to rent the property in Hampton Village I showed them. I say I will forward the lease shortly.

c) Take a short fat old man with an aura of nouveau Gucci and a tall girl with a fake Brearly accent on a brief tour of Hampton Village. The girl is very affectionate to the old man and very snooty to me. The girl is very slender but has large breasts with which she continually grazes the old man's shoulders while whispering private jokes. The couple, no doubt as transient as the summer rentals, seeks a "July retreat from . . ."—here the words become mumbled. I help them find a suitable niche where those big breasts can be fondled for nine hundred dollars a week.

d) Daydream of horny but self-denying moments of solar physics by the sea. He is explaining. I am trying to understand. His intelligence, his chipped tooth, and my knowledge of the warm stuff inside his bathing suit form a perfect balance of sense and sensibility.

Mr. Harrison's secretary, Gloria, tells me, joyful tears hanging in her eyes, that she and her boyfriend have finally set the date for their wedding. It is to be a "September affair" and I am to be invited. Gloria asks my opinion regarding color coordination of maids of honor and flowers and I pretend to agree with her choice. She is going to have a big reception at Maple Hill, a nonchic but moderately well-appointed country club just west of the Hamptons. I think of my own small house wedding held so long ago. This elicits no romantically tinted memories of Stuart, but instead for my early childhood and the days when my mother and father were less gray and more playful.

Call Mrs. Bennett. She will be happy to sit, and certainly eager to cook, on Saturday. Stuart, who does not understand, but is nevertheless *understanding* about my desire to spend a day in Manhattan and a night with my parents, is willing to take care of the children Saturday night and Sunday morning. He is dependable, but I know the task will be a strain. Stuart is all adult. His childlights having dimmed, he will find it difficult to play with John and Laura, who will probably try to engage him in a game of Sorry! or Monopoly. Maybe in ten years, when John and Laura are ready to discuss the stock market, he will be ready for a genuinely shared experience.

Late at night, when he is reviewing papers he brought home from the office, Stuart asks for a cup of coffee. He compliments me on the mellowness of the coffee and appears to be comfortable and happy sitting at his desk. I wish he were devious or mean, or at least a little suspicious. There would be something to absorb the shock wave of guilt that crashes against my infidelity.

Friday:
After tennis, stock up on groceries and good will. Macadamia

nuts for Stuart. Potato chips, against my better judgment, for John. Fudge swirl ice cream for Laura.

Saturday, early A.M.:

Shower. Long and hot. Scrub my crotch as energetically as I do before my yearly visit to the gynecologist. Then apply body lotion. I am ready for love or a Papp smear. Trouble is, as soon as the process is completed, my belly starts revving up and I know that before long my juices will start oozing and gone will be the effect of my lovely *cunta rasa.*

6

I was filled with excitement. Intuitive love is a hypothesis. Experience is proof of the pudding. I couldn't wait to begin the investigation.

I decided to rely on the sometimes capricious L.I.R.R. rather than put up with the hassles of driving. Stuart took me to the station, and as I boarded the rickety 8:56 and waved a self-conscious goodbye, I saw him rummaging through my underwear drawer and discovering my diaphragm was missing. "So long! Have fun with the kids!"

There weren't many passengers on the old train. I chose an unscarred seat next to an uncracked window and made myself comfortable. I gave the conductor a twenty dollar bill and he shook his head. I apologized.

I looked out of the dusty window as the flat potato farmland bounced before my eyes. Speonk, first stop. Just south of the tracks lived the poor, the laborers, the blacks. Below, lived the men with briefcases and the children who took lessons. Below them, the doctors, the real estate agents, the summer sailors, the sometime minglers with the Summer People. And below *them*, on the shore of Moriches Bay, the old gold.

We lurched ahead. Just west of the Hamptons we passed through the transitional zone, where the studied New England picture started to change into the look of the rural midwest. Eastport, East Moriches, Center Moriches—the southern coast of the Island began to give into its natural bent, becoming scrubbier, less verdant. I took out my book and settled back.

In Babylon, ninety pages of *The Honourable Schoolboy* later, a weary lady with a two-year old nose-runner sat down in front of me, and for the rest of the trip the little girl kept popping up and making faces at me. I wasn't sure whether she wanted to be my friend or scare me. I said hello to her once and she smiled slyly.

As we traveled further and further west and the population became denser, both in and out of the train, I couldn't seem to concentrate on anything but my *own* intrigue, so I stowed LeCarré's in my big tan shoulder bag and withdrew a small mirror to see how my face was holding up. I looked a little pale and I applied some of my lip gloss to my cheeks.

I glanced down at myself. Beneath my jacket, my simple skinny-top was clinging nicely and went well with the blue and orange paisley print skirt. My "suntan" pantyhose and my blue shoes with rope wedges and ankle-ties looked good on my freshly shaved legs.

How easy it is to be overly concerned with oneself as an object. I wasn't out to sell myself as a commodity, but I didn't want to have a greasy nose either. But where to draw the line? I remembered crying and applauding Kate in *Summer Before the Dark,* and admiring the intelligent-looking, grey-haired lady on the book jacket. But I knew that I would have touched up those gray hairs and heightened the color of my cheeks with a "natural" blusher before having my photograph taken. Was it because I wasn't sure of my accomplishments and my intelligence? Was it because I couldn't see myself ceding to age?

Admit it. I wanted Gil to have an erection in the main lobby of the Metropolitan.

The little girl in front of me popped up and glared at me as if she knew, and her mother, for the first time, pulled her down and demanded that she stop "fidgeting."

It was 11:03 when we pulled into Penn Station—dingy subterranean world that reduced us to scurriers bound for appointments, deadlines, tracks—underscoring our helplessness when it came to that inevitable time of departure we'd like to scratch. It took the edge off my excitement.

But more important than the idea of ultimate futility is a rumbling stomach. I was starving. I hurried to the underground Nedicks, where I devoured a pale hot dog and drank a tepid cup of coffee.

My bag slung over my shoulder, I walked to a book store in the station where there's always a sale in progress. I discovered a book of drawings by Hans-Georg Rauch and was captivated. Pictures emerging from pictures of infinite detail: a man knitting; look closely and it is God stitching an array of mortals—myriads of tiny detailed forms, each different, crowd the page. Factories spewing forth smoke; study the streams and the swirling pollution forms graceful rows of stately trees, separated by a classic waterfall. A flimsy, flowing, lace curtain formed from thousands of minute soldiers standing at attention! Reduced to $2.95. I purchased it and made my way TO STREET and the midday bustle of W. 33rd and Seventh.

After getting my bearings (with which I always had difficulty here) I strolled to Fifth Avenue and 38th and looked at bathing suits in Lord and Taylor's. I found a brown French bikini on the fourth floor which made me feel particularly screwable, and charged it. With my L & T shopping bag containing my new suit and my new book, pacifiers for the two poles of my ego, I walked north along Fifth, feeling good. It was a beautiful day. The sun glistened on shop windows and car fenders, and the air quality seemed even more than Acceptable.

At 53rd I turned west, deciding on a visit to the Museum of Modern Art. I checked my shopping bag and went on a tour of the new exhibit—a display of taxis from around the world. An illustration of the trustees' ever-expanding definition of art. Despite the dramatic lighting and intelligent use of floor space, it reminded me of the boring afternoon I had spent with Stuart (he, consumed with interest; I, trying, and failing still, to meet his soul half-way) at the Auto Show at the New York Coliseum some time back.

But the good old standbys—Cezanne, Nolde, van Gogh, Picasso —reengaged me in lively communion. My desire to start painting again (I hadn't picked up a brush since Laura was born) was sparked, as it always was when I visited the upper floors. This time I made a vow to follow through. It was my last chance, somehow. Future promises would be considered self-deceptions. This time desire became necessity.

I returned to the main level and stood at the large window looking out at what was the familiar sculpture garden, now an area under construction. How well I remembered sitting on the patio, sipping iced tea, watching the colorful people drifting about, bending and peering, shaking heads, nodding with approval at the real and abstract renditions of themselves—the passersby reviewing the permanent collection. Trying to imagine the missing sculptured pieces in their old locations, I remembered the commanding nude figure of a woman by Lachaise, and for the first time associated it with Gladys. Big, but buoyant. I imagined Gladys standing in a studio, tennis attire discarded, legs akimbo, arms on hips, as the sculptor exaggerated her lines for reproduction, her ample ass to become poised forever in muscular stasis.

For the first time, too, I toy with the idea of Gladys as a lesbian. In graphic imagery I see her lying naked on the Har-Tru, writhing with abandoned delight as one naked woman, kneeling over her head, strokes her breasts and another, bending over her torso, spreads her legs, drives two fingers up her discharging aperture and begins mixing and stirring as if she were preparing a batter. Pinioned by these two diligent workers, Gladys comes in fitful spasms on the grainy surface of the court. I identify the cook at the cunt as none other than myself. Oh well, now that I am there I might as well take a closer look. Gladys rests for a moment as I withdraw my two fingers and gently pull apart the outer labia. I study the rosy inner lips. Exposed between the frame of coarse black hair, they look so innocent and inviting, and I am burning with curiosity. I bend to taste the soft, shiny-wet interior, and as my teeth latch onto a delectable morsel, Gladys again groans and squirms with appreciation and I marvel at my power. So who's the fucking pervert?

I focus on other matters.

An hour early at the Metropolitan, I was standing in front of Bonheur's "Horse Fair," reflecting on its enormity, when a voice from behind greeted me softly.

"Hello, Joan."

I turned around and my reflections galloped away.

"Oh—hi, Gil. I guess we're *both* early." He looked charmingly disheveled in chinos and denim shirt, collar unbuttoned, hair windblown.

"Yeah. I got hung up on a lousy paragraph on thermal equilibrium and escaped before it turned into a compulsion. How was your trip?"

"You're name dropping. What's 'thermal equilibrium'—a case of the hot flashes?"

He attempted a smile and touched his glasses. "I'm really bugged by this chapter. I can't seem to put it together properly."

Was my lip gloss smudged on a tooth? Did I suffer from unsightly dandruff? "I wish I could help, but I'm fresh out of formu—lae, is it?"

"You can help me forget about it."

"Let's sit near the fountain in the cafeteria," I suggested. "We can have some wine."

We walked together, never touching, to the cafeteria, where we sat stroking our glasses of chablis by the Fountain of the Muses. Lithe figures dancing through the rippling pool, out to inspire us with the gift of poetry and song. But Gil was about as poetic as a morose clam and Milles' graceful creatures only made me doubt the significance of our meeting. Had I deluded myself into thinking that our love-making had meant more to him than just another coitus interruptus?

"It's hard for me to shift gears," he said. "I've been working so long I'm a damn drag. Let's walk a little."

"Sure."

Within a few minutes he shook himself free of his mood and I was grateful I hadn't made it worse by probing. Passing Rembrandt's *Aristotle Before a Bust of Homer,* I playfully compared him to the great teacher and embarrassed him. "Aristotle was a great mind contemplating a small universe," he said. "I'm a small mind contemplating a great universe. Aside from that, and the beard, we're identical." He returned the compliment by comparing me to Ingres' *Odalisque,* taking great pleasure in seeing me turn red when an elderly couple overheard him and laughed. "Except for the hair style, I think it's a terrific likeness," he commented. "Wouldn't you say, dear?" The flawless nude seemed to be looking straight at me, her seductive glance clearly turning to disdain before my very eyes. The bitch.

We moved on.

Stopping before Yves Tanguy's *Mirage le Temps,* I touched Gil's shoulder. It was our first contact. "Is this what the landscape of your ideas looks like?" I asked, the question drawing emphasis away from the gesture. In the foreground of the painting was a very precisely rendered group of indefinables resembling bones and pieces of machinery. They were set on a vast stretch of substance that looked like fluid sand. "If you could transpose those astronomical truths of yours into art, what would they look like?"

"Beethoven's *Fifth.*"

"And I always figured it was Mozart. You live and learn. Tell me, Sir Isaac, do you feel any closer to the bottom line since you've been probing the heavens? Think I can count on the old epistemological conundrum? You know—we're trapped within the mode of human thought and therefore the absolute is forever elusive? Rendering you just as dumb as me?"

He took my hand briefly. The act was as much of a statement as his words. "No such luck. I have faith," he said, "that it all amounts to more than a lot of cerebral masturbation, that we get hints of the ultimate stuff. If all knowledge is linked with our mental gyrations we can at least *point* toward the absolute."

"In the patterns of your scientific data do you see some kind of cohering agent? Or are you a 'big bang' purist?"

"It's hard for me *not* to wonder about there being some unifying—impetus—in the laws of a changing universe, something besides mass and energy. At least I can't help but see an aesthetic inherent in it all. The more science invades my fantasy, the more inventive reality seems." There was a loveable innocence in his tone.

I stroked his side. He emanated such warmth. What would I do if someone I knew saw me now? The chance meeting was a possibility, not a danger. I was too comfortable to care. "Starting to understand something like the Saturn rings makes not only the universe seem more fantastic to me, but reason itself seems more awesome," I said. "Yours, anyway." The moment was mental, but his musky smell still beckoned to me through his denim shirt. "We're steering clear of the word 'intelligence' to describe the possible form contiguous to matter," I said. "Don't want to force it to be human."

"We'd be talking about mercy, punishment, all the conventional traits."

"If there's a force transcendent to the created, its intelligence is sure to be unintelligible to *me*, at least."

"Unless its nature is *so* simple it defies theorization."

I couldn't help making comparisons. Stuart was a skeptic whose doubt was doctrine. Gil's uncertainties were touched with reverence. Stuart's metaphysical bent was mechanistic, like his love-making. Gil's was aesthetic, inspirited. I looked into his face and he disarmed me with a crooked smile. Rallying, "You've got ontological humility," I quipped.

"Sounds like a disease, but thanks anyway," he replied. "Say, do you have something you'd like to get done while you're here in town?"

"Maybe I can pick up some stuff at Central Art Supply while I'm here. We can meet later if you like."

He threw me a darting look. "Why? Don't you want me to come with you?"

"Yes, but I thought maybe you would rather—"

"Well, I wouldn't. Let's go."

It turned out to be a good idea. Gil had parked in the Museum's lot on 80th and Fifth, and we drove to the art store, miraculously found a place to park, and spent half an hour poking around the place. It was thrilling just to be handling the materials again. The charcoal! The tubes! The spiral pads! I forgot that I would be taking the train home the next day and bought too much to carry.

We were loaded down with paints, brushes, pads, disposable palettes, canvas, stretchers, and other aids to gratification when we returned to the car.

"What am I going to do with all this?"

"I'll drive you back tomorrow."

I refused his offer, and we agreed that he would bring my supplies to his cottage when he moved in for the summer. I'd pick them up there.

"Which reminds me, I've got your lease with me."

"How efficient. Let's go up to my apartment. I'm making dinner for us—or is it lunch—and you can see how efficient *I* can be."

"I assumed you could only open cans."

"I'm full of surprises."

We parked the car on 121st and walked three blocks to his apartment building with my bags. It took a few minutes to open the three locks to 5B. One of them worked a rod which rammed into a floor fitting, he said. I thought of the door to my house beyond whose flimsy lock my kids were probably battling now in relative safety from all dangers but each other.

"Ever think of this as a war zone?" I asked.

"I'm a fatalist. But then, I never forget to lock the door."

I was hoping he wouldn't become agitated about his work. I imagined that it was there waiting for us on an old oak desk, its stellar secrets ready to harass us for the rest of the afternoon.

I was wrong about the oak desk. A portable typewriter holding what I assumed to be a page on thermal equilibrium was stationed on a long black conference table—the kind that I'd expect to see in a business office—against a wall in the living room.

Papers, magazines, books, mail were piled on and under the table. Assorted bookcases lined most of the room, packed with volumes of science, art, history. Horizontal heaps of *Fantasy and Science Fiction, Analog,* and *Scientific American* were amassed on the top shelves.

Above the conference table hung a bulletin board with push-pinned scribbled notes and printed matter. Next to it hung a large aluminum-framed reproduction of one of my favorite Magritte's —*La Condition Humaine.* With mystical clarity it shows a scene resting on an easel before an open window. This painting within the painting depicts exactly that part of the landscape outside the window blocked out by the canvas. The perfect juxtaposition raises the dilemma of distinguishing the real from the retinal, erasing the distinction between reality and the mind's perception of reality. (Stuart never liked any of Magritte's paintings: "Too eerie. They give me the creeps.")

I could see that a vacuum cleaner had recently left its impressions in the chocolate brown wall-to-wall shag, and the vague odor of furniture polish hung in the air. Had Gil cleaned the apartment just for me? I arranged my bags alongside the tweedy sofa and realized that it had been quite some time since I had peed.

I walked through an open archway into the kitchen-dining room area. "Charming."

"Small."

I hesitated. "Would you tell me where the bathroom is?"

He led me to a white door next to the bedroom. "The lay-out is similar to the place in Hampton Village, don't you think?"

"Except this is nicer, and cozier." God, I had to go! "Would you excuse me for a minute?"

Life's small embarrassments: a fart, a burp, a tinkle, and a flush. I was determined to have an open, honest relationship with Gil, and made an effort not to let my first audible stream and loud gurgle of plumbing affect my poise.

I emerged from the bathroom with an air of nonchalance and Gil smiled guilelessly. I knew then that nothing, not even the advancement of solar physics, would come between us that afternoon.

"Do you like veal with marsala? Say yes, because that's what I'm making for you," he advised, rolling up his sleeves.

"Of course I do. What can I do to help?"

"You sit there and give me moral support. Or else you wash the lettuce."

There are some hungers that gnaw at you until you appease them. I discovered there are others that don't make themselves known until they are gratified. Watching Gil prepare our meal in his small kitchen I realized how I had been starved for this kind of attention. I was enraptured as he scoured the refrigerator for a lemon, scooped out the flour, pounded the veal, sliced off a slab of butter, rinsed the wine glasses. Every small act seemed to be dedicated to me. When he said "Hand me the salt, it's on the table over there, hon," I melted like the butter in the frying pan. Anything more than opening a can of diet soda was traditionally a feminine act in my house. Stuart was unsettled by any function he deemed housewifely. Not that he ever said as much, but on the rare occasion, as for example when I was sick, that he had to put through a wash or squeeze an orange, he felt compromised. As I broke up the lettuce into bite sized pieces and Gil reduced the heat under the veal and marsala, I felt a communion I had never known, the mundane setting being one of its cozy components. When he wiped his floury hands on a dish towel he appeared so profoundly masculine I thought my legs would buckle.

"I think I'd like to be sick just to have you feed me chicken soup," I said. "Would you?" I was peeling a cucumber.

"My repertoire is limited. Who makes chicken soup!" He was

68

reaching into the pantry for a box of instant rice and turned to me in mock amazement. The answer was yes, he would feed me.

We sat opposite each other at the small table in the dining cove and Gil poured the red wine. "To what shall we toast?" he asked, raising his glass and leaning towards me.

To your tongue. To your hands. To your prick. "To a perfect performance," I paraphrased. "Hollander's, that is."

"I shouldn't have asked. We'll drink to us."

As we ate we talked about matters that curiosity and upbringing would have us review. It was not enough that our smells and sounds and streams of consciousness were mutually agreeable. Society required that we embellish our primal beings with historical placement. His voice caressed me, his eyes reached into my soul, his hands set me on fire, his view of the universe enthralled me, but, getting down to brass tacks, I had no idea how many traffic violations he had committed or whether his parents were living or dead.

As a guide to enlightenment we ask about the trappings of our lives. Subject as they are to misinterpretation and misdesignation, we know they might obstruct an otherwise fresh perception we have of each other, but we plod on in our search for the truth. I winced, for example, when he told me he had lived with a woman for a few years—an instructor of Latin at Hunter. I immediately constructed a *Playboy* centerfold with a mind like a steel trap. He told me that her most outstanding quality was her persuasive aggressiveness, that she was the first woman to force the ecstasies from the agonies of adolescence.

"She's fourteen years older than I am. At Amherst, and then Columbia, I was very shy with girls. Betsy gave me tea and sympathy and took me under her wing. She landed a better teaching position at Florida State and took it. She left me when I turned seventeen, which was somewhere around my twenty-ninth birthday."

I told Gil about my "coming out" experiences at Vassar, the shortcomings of my marriage, and Laura and John. While I masked my petty jealousies, recognizing them to be functions of my immaturity, Gil became downright peevish when I spoke about my family. Sometime in the future, I thought, maybe this will trouble me. At the time it was a foible I found very endearing. It reflected agitation, possessiveness, unreasonableness, all of which I felt perversely in need of. Stuart's damned reasonableness boardered on disinterest. True, I was free to do as I pleased, barring sexual transgression. But this independence had not been granted out of warm regard, but rather out of benign neglect.

"I know your type," I said. "You captivate the class with your deep voice and mastery of the subject. You give fatherly advice and as long as the professorial role is maintained you're hot stuff. You make a terrific mentor. But beneath the surface lies the jellied confidence of an innocent star gazer."

He laughed. "You really think I'm a schmuck, don't you?"

"Just bordering." I rose, leaned over the table and kissed him lightly on the mouth. "I love being here."

"Can I help it if I like to think that the day we met is the day you were born? What can I say? Some aspects of my personality just haven't developed," he grinned. "Bear with me?"

I nodded, stroking his calf with my foot under the table. "But maybe not forever."

"That's what you think."

"What do you like about me, anyway?" I asked, looking for reassurance rather than itemization.

"The way you look, the way you feel, the way you make *me* feel."

"That's *it?*" I smiled.

"Also, you're a smartass, which is apparently good therapy for me. Why do you like *me?*"

While I finished chewing a morsel of veal I thought about it. "It does seem odd, and don't laugh at me, but you put a kind of visceral *go* into my aspirations. Do you understand? Not to mention the inspiration you put into my viscera, which is to say I think you're sexy."

"I'm not laughing." He reached across the table and cupped his hand over my face briefly, then withdrew.

70

I took another sip of wine. "I suppose you think I'm an uninhibited bitch, but this is new to me. Really. Before I met you—"

"You were a virgin?" he smiled.

I looked at his fingers tracing patterns on his wine glass, wishing it were me. Do I tell him I had ass in my heart but no heart in my ass? "Well, so to speak, yes," I answered. "You do know what I mean."

"I don't know if I believe you, but I want to," he said, looking down at his plate.

Yielding sensations were spreading across my thighs and up into my belly, urging me to drop the subject and possibly my pants. "Why are you sitting so far away?" I exchanged my chair for his lap and bit his ear. "That's better." I speared the last piece of meat on his plate and fed it to him, stealing a scrap of it with a kiss.

An inviting elevation was straining against his trousers and I pressed my left buttock against it. We kissed again.

"For dessert," he muttered against my face, "you have a choice of coffee cake, butter pecan—"

"I'll have the speciality of the house," I interrupted, demonstrating with a sucking kiss to the delicious little scar on the side of his neck.

He lifted my shirt and bra over my breasts in one deft movement and attached his lips to a nipple. We wrapped our arms around each other and all perceptions converged into our expectant mass. The warm glow of contentment I had felt with a baby at my breast was diversified. Embracing me with his strong arms as no baby had done, he made me feel as though I were giving nourishment and being made secure at the same time. Then, too, because it was Gil's roving kiss, not the blind sucking of a hungry baby, I sank into the action at my breast as pure pleasure in itself, the sensations fanning out to all parts of my body, adding sexual urgency to the protective exchange. There was such a sweet stirring of roles between us—mother, father, baby, lover—like a changing sea of tenderness.

He carried me to his bed where we tasted and explored each

other with exquisite thoroughness. With no one else had I exposed my desires with such honesty, entrusted them so completely to another's care. We had no tradition of propriety between us, no curtain of judgment. The desire he felt for me made me dizzy with the impact of my existence. Through his eyes I saw myself afresh.

He was lying on me, quickening the drive, when the ineffable climax came, and I was lost in the eruption.

"Angel cake," he whispered into my neck after the beating had subsided.

"You're delicious."

"You are too."

"Parfait."

His legs on mine. His pelvis on mine. His chest on mine. His body leaning on mine in heavy rest. So comforting. I moved, just enough to feel his fur rub against my belly.

He encircled me with his arms and pressed his warm thighs hard against mine. How sheltered I felt. "Come back with me later and stay with me tonight."

"My parents are expecting me. What will I say to—"

"Please."

"Yes. . . . Of course."

7

Gil was dressing in the bedroom when I called my parents from the kitchen wall phone.

"I think I'll be staying here in Manhattan tonight, Mom."

"Why, dear?"

"I'm with a friend from college—we're going to a concert. She invited me to stay over."

"We were looking forward to seeing you."

"But this friend—"

"Who? Nancy what's-her-married-name moved to New Jersey last year. Who are you still friendly with?"

"Linda Colson."

"The same Linda Colson who never returned your hair dryer?"

"Forgiveness is a virtue, ma."

"What's her number in case I want to call you?"

My mother and I were friends. We used to share our clothes. Honesty struggled to gain possession of my tongue.

I gave her Gil's number. "I . . . uh . . . can't reach Stuart right now. If he gets in touch with you, would you tell him where I am?"

"But won't you be—"

"I bought some art supplies today, Mom. I'm going to paint again, finally."

"Joan! That's wonderful!" She reported the news to my father and he took the receiver from her.

"You don't know how happy that makes me feel," he said. "I never said anything, but every time I look at that little oil of yours in our bedroom I think of how a talent is going to waste."

"Well, whatever there is is going to be put to the test."

"Good luck."

"Thanks."

I would have liked to share the news of another beginning with them, but I knew that however well we knew each other, this was one turning point my parents might learn of only in retrospect, if ever.

Hollander's technique was superb; his interpretation divine. At least that's what *The New York Times* said the next day. Frankly, with my insides all warm and creamy, with Gil's head leaning towards mine, his mint-cool breath brushing my cheek, I didn't much care.

A fitting quotation was printed on the program, elucidating the Andante Expressivo movements of the Brahms Sonata in F minor:

Now gleams in the gloaming the pale moonlight,
and there two loving hearts unite
in ecstacy bound together.
Sternau

We waited through the Scherzo, the Intermezzo, and Finale for the intermission, when I whispered, my lips tickling his ear, "Let's fugue," and we left, Molto Vivace, for his apartment.

The movement is Sustenuto. We sit face to face on the floor of the living-room, the brown shag brushing up between our buttocks, our hands playing between each other's thighs. His fingers

74

strumming the cleft, always aching for more; his eyes, half-curtained, staring down at the effects of his manipulations; I, gently cupping his balls in my hands, stroking them with my thumbs.

Watching his fingers caressing and becoming gummy with my secretions, I move closer to him, spreading my thighs further apart, pushing against his fingers in a flurry of staccato attacks.

The bow of his back curves towards me. He looks into my face and I feel as though I am breathing in his image more than seeing it.

His warm wet hands slide along my thighs and over my back, pulling me towards him. I embrace his shoulders, and move still closer, until my nipples are barely brushing his chest. Our lips touch. He pushes past my tongue with his and we suck at each other, drawing the current of pleasure up from our loins, returning it recharged, creating a cycle of urgency.

We move closer. My breasts are pressed against his chest; my thighs, against his hips. We encircle each other.

He slips his hands between us and guides his instrument into the pit. A groan issues up from my depths. Crescendo, crescendo.

But wait—I want to see us fused together before the cymbals crash. Don't move! "Let me look!" I gasp.

Breathing hard, sphincter contracting, I try to control, to stay still, poised before the onrushing finale in an ecstasy of deprivation.

We examine our bodies, connecting, his dense hair mingling with my dewy bush. We try not to move.

I am awed by the painful pressure of what is coming. We can not hold still for long. His head is thrown back and he grimaces in mindless abandon. Caught by the rhythm of sensation we move together with percussive strength, surrendering to the last insistent measures.

Afterwards, we split a can of tuna fish and a glass of orange juice, and got into bed.

We slid under the sheet and drew the comforter up around us. We shared the warmth of our radiating bodies in a tired-sweet embrace, his thigh tucked up between my legs, softly pressing, his cheek gently bristling against my collar bone, his lips touching my neck, his tousled hair personalized by his own subtle musk.

He reached out and turned off the light and for a little while we lay listening to our breathing and the quiet sounds of our bodies moving against each other, finding untouched places to settle into. I was flooded with tenderness.

Tracing circles on my shoulder, he said, "When we first met this afternoon I seemed a little bothered, didn't I?"

"I was afraid you were having second thoughts."

"What an idiot. It was—"

"The chapter that you were working on, I hope?"

"An excuse. I saw you in front of that painting and I got mad."

"In front of the Bonheur? Great. You think I'm horsey."

"Don't laugh at me. I just had the feeling that I was being used. That you were in town for a couple of hours to take in some culture and a kinky lay."

"I don't believe it. Isn't this supposed to be a variation on *my* theme, if anybody's?"

"You don't belong to me and I keep thinking, well, that your mind will wander."

"Where will it go?" I asked.

"To bed with your husband. For a lesson in comparative anatomy."

"Gil! You're not going to do that, are you? You're above that."

"I'm not above anything."

I held him close. "I told you how it is. No interrogations, okay?"

"All right, all right. I'm sorry. What can I tell you? If I had an analyst he'd say that because my father died when I was young, leaving an overprotective mother and sister to heap unqualified adoration on me, I was totally unprepared to deal with the affections of a woman whose status, by definition, precludes the notion of absolute love."

76

"You deserve an Emmy for that one," I said. "Is it true?"

"Who knows if it's true. It sounds good, doesn't it?" He nuzzled into my neck. "I love you."

I kissed his head.

"Don't let me screw it up," he said. "We fit together. In every way. Do you love me?"

For a moment I enjoyed listening to the question hanging in the silence, and then, resting my leg on top of his, answered, "Yes, I do."

Something fell to the uncarpeted floor above us (a chair? a radio?) but the noise of others sealed us into our own privacy.

I rubbed my foot along his calf.

Time seemed to flow through us, as if we lay outside its laws.

I imagined us snuggled in a protective bubble drifting away, deathless and alone.

"I wish things were simpler," he said.

There. I noticed the lamp shade was crooked and we were no longer in the center of the universe.

"I wish you didn't have to leave."

With death inevitable, an old fear of absence and loss returned. Euphoria was tainted. The image of two children, far away, love-woven into my soul, compensating.

"Let's not think now," I whispered. "Let's sleep a little."

He said nothing. He lay on his back beside me, space between us.

I woke up in the middle of the night disoriented—a creature of habit confused by the displacement of windows and walls. I was in bed alone.

In the semi-darkness I found Gil's shirt draped over a chair. I pressed it to my face and inhaled the faint odor he had left in it. Chilled, I put the shirt over my naked body and buttoned it. The sleeves were too long and I rolled them up two cuffs.

I tiptoed cautiously out of the bedroom, wanting to come upon him the way I've stumbled on a beautiful shell or colored sea glass on the beach.

I walked through the hallway, past the bathroom. I was coming to the kitchen area when I saw him. He was sitting, his back towards me, at his desk at the far end of the living room, bending over something illuminated by a small table lamp. He was wearing a blue and green plaid robe which had fallen open, leaving his left leg exposed, loosely extending out from the chair.

I stood very still, not wanting to disturb the picture.

Oh, what a clit-stirring limb! How gently the thigh and calf muscles curved out from the angular knee. How the long line of muscle was made even more inviting by the curly tufts of hair, giving the leg a texture that had to be touched, kissed, rubbed against the smooth skin of a belly, a breast—mine!

Watching him bathed in the soft light of the small table lamp, as an exercise of will I made myself stand outside the scene for just a few seconds longer, etching it.

(I can bring out of storage bits from long ago accompanied by the precisely remembered mode of childhood objectivity. My teacher's lined face smiling down at me against the backdrop of blackboard arithmetic. My mother, frozen in the act of tucking under the sheet with the faded yellow and blue roses. Mundane instants captured specifically for future reference and, like time capsules, they create a totally premeditated fusion of my past and my future.)

The image recorded (will I perceive it on my deathbed?), I spoke. "You're up early."

He turned abruptly, startled. "Hey! How long were you standing there?" He tossed off his glasses. "What were you doing—*appraising* me?"

"Oh, Gil!" I came towards him and he softened.

"I didn't mean that. You look nice in the shirt. Did I wake you up?"

"No. But I'm disturbing *you.*"

"I like that."

I sat down on his lap and put my arms around his neck. "Are you resolving the thermal equilibrium thing?"

"I did," he answered, encircling my waist.

I glanced down at his notes. I made out "mean molecular

78

weight" and "specific heat" but the rest of it—the equations with the open p's and the cut off t's—made no sense at all.

"I'm snowed."

He pressed me to his body. "Do you know I started working tonight so I could pretend I had time to squander? That you were a permanent fixture I could take for granted?"

"You might get bored."

"What a luxury."

I leaned back against the desk. "What will it be?" I flung open my arms. "Your advancement on me or the advancement of science?"

"Same thing." I felt him hardening under me as he opened one of the shirt buttons, and another.

"You certainly can rise to the occasion."

He grinned and his hand slipped into the opening of the shirt and touched my breast. "So smooth," he whispered.

The edge of the desk was digging into the small of my back. I rose from his lap, slipping away from his hand. I pushed his papers aside. I sat on the edge of the desk and lay back on its hard surface. My toes were barely touching the floor. My body was arched and stretched and vulnerable. "Do something."

Gil stood up, moved the chair away. His robe fell open.

The shirt on me had twisted to one side and an eager tit was poking out from the unbuttoned section of it. It was center stage, the light from the table lamp shining directly on it. It sang out for a hand and Gil accommodated it. He gently massaged the helpless globe, then bent to kiss its peak, creating eddies of pleasure tingling. His hand ran over my clothed belly, reached the end of the shirt and glided underneath. It stroked and pinched my belly and furry patch, and I tried to lift and spread my legs to bare the wet center, but couldn't.

"Help me," I begged, and he understood. He placed his hands under my knees and raised my legs, standing between them, bending them up and apart, until my heels rested on the edge of the desk on either side of him. Slowly, with deliberation, his open hands traveled from under my knees, gracefully down along my inner thighs, to merge at the overhanging shirttail. He lifted it,

79

revealing the hidden lips, and went on stroking my thighs, his thumbs meeting at their center, pulling apart the labia and dancing and probing between them.

I closed my eyes. His thumbs rubbed and rolled the hot nib. They pressed inside against the gummy smooth walls—spreading them, drawing them together, prying open, pressing together, stretching and holding open, exposing the dark moist chamber to light and air. My mouth opened in agonized delight. Then I could feel his hands separating, moving up along my thighs until they were braced under my knees, pushing them further apart and back towards the wall, the slit opening.

And suddenly his fat hard cock was within the gates, striking the cervix as I muffled a cry of pain. He slipped his hands under my shoulders and lifted me up towards him. Aching, I wrapped my legs around his waist and reached for his shoulders.

He held me to him and we kissed, tasting nighttime's bitterness. He took a few steps, his hands supporting my ass, pushing it against his pelvis again and again.

I teetered on the brink of release, then backed off until I was left with sensations of localized pressure and static abrasiveness.

As he ejaculated, I was close to rejoicing in my disappointment. This had been the first time in my life when failure to experience orgasm was devoid of accusation. Self- or other-directed doubt was inappropriate. The angle of entry had been a little off, perhaps? It didn't matter. What did matter was its insignificance.

It was a gratification I kept to myself.

We toasted a couple of English muffins and brewed some tea and sat together like old friends, slouching at the dining room table. For once, I was not distracted by my importunate vulva.

He sipped his tea, and toyed with a toasted crumb. "I feel married."

"Already?"

"We had a contracted courtship, didn't we? Why are you looking at me like that?" he frowned. (My head was tilted to one side and I was smiling.)

80

"I like being with you when you need a shave." I stroked his bristly cheek with the back of my hand and he took my hand and kissed my fingers.

"Stay with me sometime, after I move into the house."

"If I get a mother's helper, then the chil—"

"Don't talk about your family, now. I can keep your paint supplies and you can work at my place."

I looked into his sleepy eyes. "I'd love to paint with you working and—just knocking around. All right. We'll evade."

"Let's go back to bed. I want to wake up with you."

We cleared the table and returned to the bedroom. He took off his robe, and I, the shirt. We slipped under the comforter and embraced tenderly, without the urgent direction of passion. Each kiss, each touch, we savored as a delicacy. His hand cupping my breast, a gesture of simple affection; my hand stroking his balls, an act of reverence. Exploration became a game of curiosity, open-ended, of infinite variety and concern, of quiet absorption in contours and textures.

We fell asleep, our legs entwined, my breasts resting against his open arm.

I got up early, a whirlwind of nervous energy. No time to luxuriate. I had to make a train. It was as if I'd been missing for a month. *They* were worrying, panicking, suspecting. The laundry, the mail, the dust, the crumbs, the dirty dishes. They'll take one look at me and *know*! On the other hand: the bastards, couldn't they put through a lousy wash?

As the train pulled away in the underground gloom Gil, awkwardly changing stances there on the gray platform, looked like an abandoned child. I felt a strong affection for him. At the same time I was uneasy, fearing discovery, exposure, scorn. By Sayville, this anxiety neatly merged with my general panic about my children's piano engagement scheduled for that afternoon. I vividly remembered sitting before an audience of relatives and critics, reaching for the pedal, listening to the silence that I had to break, and suddenly becoming overwhelmed with the fear of Forgetting or Stumbling, wishing, with all the passion of childhood, that it was already Tomorrow.

John and Laura sat, along with Mrs. Stern's seventeen other pupils, in the segregated front rows of the audience, right up close to the big bad Baldwin. Mrs. Stern, a scarecrow of a woman with a mass of jet black hair framing her face, and looking rather like a smiling quarter note, hovered on the sidelines. Every year on a Sunday at 4:00 Mrs. Stern held her annual recital in her home, filling her living and dining rooms with rented bridge chairs and preparing butter cookies and punch to serve after the marathon event. Every year she would inform her students that they were limited to two guests each, but every year there were grandparents and other lovers of the performing arts that she couldn't possibly turn away at the door. As a result, a number of guests occupied standing room only—shifting their weight from one foot to another, leaning on walls, eyeing the punch and cookies, and no doubt becoming increasingly hostile as the afternoon wore on. I had been a guest on several occasions. Once when Gladys's daughter was taking lessons I filled the father slot, he being in bed with the flu. Once I came at the behest of Mrs. Stern herself. It was the year we had struck up a conversation at a P.T.A. meeting and she had discovered that I liked Gustav Mahler's *First Symphony*. What her recital had in common with Gustav Mahler I'll never know, unless it was the fact that Stuart would have been unable to sit through either of them.

This was John's and Laura's first recital. They were to appear early in the program because Mrs. Stern always had the beginners play before the advanced students. I sat in the fifth row center, martyred. There was no way I could possibly extract myself from the audience without making a spectacle of myself. Stuart stood to the rear, ready with his camera to photograph his children and slip away unnoticed. I was afraid the flashbulbs would startle Laura and John while they were playing, but

Stuart, not being a mother, had no such qualms and was not about to accommodate mine.

I was the perfect model of a neurotic, feeling as one with my squirming babies in the first row. Surreptitiously, I dug the fingernails of my right hand into my left forearm to distract me from the anxiety of the approaching ordeal. I was locked in this grip of maternal madness until Mrs. Stern began the speech in which she thanked her guests for coming and made little jokes about her pupils to lighten the mood: "Cindy Heffler broke her right leg last week and she's here today only because I promised her you'd all sign her cast. Rodney Schaefer is playing Debussy's *Arabesque* rather than his *Little Shepherd* as listed on the program, because Rodney says it's more of a challenge." As Mrs. Stern rambled on, the muscles in my right hand relaxed and I no longer needed one pain to distract me from another. Her mellow tones broke the trajectory of my single-minded gaze, and I found myself attending to members of the audience, then looking at a sketch of Mozart hanging above the mantel, then looking through the portrait and into Gil's apartment. He was working at his desk. I bent over him and kissed his head. He rose and took my hand and I led him to the seat next to mine, and throughout the recital the engrossed mother to my right had no idea that she was sharing her place with the specter of my love.

The nervousness I felt about Laura's and John's performing was both an echo of my own childhood fears as well as the striking of a familiar chord—maternal distress. Gil played in a section of my emotional orchestra for whose instruments I had only read the score, never heard the music. My heart was divided, then, as I sat beside his phantasm, watching Laura step up to the piano, adjust the chair with poise, and prepare to take her place among the immortals. With Gil near me I was not quite the woman Laura knew, and, as that new woman, my perspective of her was altered. I was more than her mother. I was a lover.

My concentration was keen, but my fear had softened to concern, as Laura took one fleeting glance at the audience, turned

83

towards the piano, raised her small hands above the keyboard, and began her performance. A flashbulb went off, objectifying the image of the little girl in blue denim plucking her way through "Up in the Sky," and with it, I experienced a cognitive jolt. The child appeared as Other, a totality apart from myself. She sat stiffly, close to the piano, elbows held in towards her body. Her fingers moved slowly, cautiously, the pinkies curling away from the keys. She was not a reflection of the woman who watched from the fifth row, who remembered sitting on the edge of an upholstered pianobench, her teacher urging her always to sit closer, to play with more deliberation.

It was not a change in attitude or point of view. It was an existential rupture. It had the quality of a time warp, for I could see the little girl in blue denim as a woman, with secrets and schedules to which I was not privy, nor cared to be. My being was severed from hers.

Aware of my singularity, I was at once apprehensive and exhilarated. It was as if the very fact of my motherhood had been filling out my identity. I was afraid to lose its substance, but eager to explore my new contours. As I sat watching Laura complete her second piece, I felt a tremendous rush of passion—for Gil, for my dry brushes and unopened oils, for my replenishing joys.

When John was pumping and swaying his way through "On Yonder Rock Reclining," Laura, settled again in the first row, turned toward me, seeking approval for her own performance. I mouthed "Very good!" and was repaid with a familiar little smile—very proper, meant to be grown-up, but failing to hide the childish glee lighting up her face. The rupture of being had passed. Laura was my baby again, and John, still. The resumption of my maternity did not negate that lusty sense of self that I had attained. On the contrary, it put it in a setting, like a precious stone.

8

As the days went by I became less and less interested in deriving pleasure from my relationship with Stuart, and it became more and more deficient. I even went so far as to drop my vaginal exercise as a means of self-arousal, but Stuart never complained of dry entry and was soon lubricating himself, in private of course, before coming to bed. Our union deteriorated to fact devoid of fancy, consent without agreement.

My secret life thrived on the vitamins I withheld from my ailing marriage, and every laugh lost added joy to my soul and helped justify my breach of contract. Stuart, if he noticed my negligence, said or hinted at nothing. However, since I knew he would hardly initiate a discussion on so sensitive an issue as sexual default, I interpreted his increased irritability as an expression of concern over my being remiss in that delicate area. He addressed himself to items such as my attire, with, for example, "You have a closet full of clothes. Why do you always have to wear that dungaree skirt, may I ask?"

The quality about me that had attracted Stuart before we were married, a certain freedom of style and expression, became the object of his criticism. Years ago he probably had thought that his admiration would turn to emulation, but it hadn't. It had only turned to annoyance as he grew stuffier. Now that he more than likely felt that something important had gone awry in our relationship, petty annoyances became less tolerable—were beginning, in fact, to gall.

I could easily deal with Stuart's ill humor, but I wasn't sure of how I'd fare in dealing with his suspicions. Nevertheless I took a few chances (one big one) before Gil moved into the summer house. I saw him once when I traveled into the City on one of the buses chartered by the Village Church to enable deprived East Enders to shop and take in a Wednesday matinee. And I saw him again for what I thought would be a brazen, blazing Saturday matinee in my bedroom.

Stuart was in New Jersey, visiting a client, and John and Laura were in Scarsdale, visiting Stuart's parents, from where they would return shampooed, scrubbed, and brainwashed into thinking that accountancy was the only respectable profession in America.

Our little *tete à tail* was not without complications, however, because we were interrupted by a telephone call from my mother-in-law.

We had just begun frolicking on my sanctified sheets. My skirt was crumpled around my waist. My little silk panties were dangling from an ankle, and Gil was lying on me, gnawing hungrily at my crotch. His gray and white striped shirt was wrinkled around his chest. His dungarees and shorts were dropped below his knees and I was happily sucking on his lively cock, which was just swelling to its maximum proportions when the phone rang.

"Don't answer it!" Gil gasped from between my legs.

"I have to! It might be an emergency!" (I've never been able to let a phone ring when the children are not at home.)

It rang again. "Don't!" Gil repeated. But I managed to reach for the receiver.

"Heeeeloo," the nasal voice gaily cooed.

Oh, well, at least I knew the children were all right.

From my awkward position it was difficult to answer normally. "Hello, Sara," I said to the receiver and to the organ pressed against it. "How are things?"

"Wonderful," came the reply. "We're just having a ball here."

"Who is that?" whispered Gil to my thigh.

I held the phone's mouthpiece against the mattress. "My mother-in-law," I said, and watched his penis diminish in size.

"I'm glad you're having a good time," I said into the mouthpiece, developing the urge to laugh.

"George and I took them to Temple today. They liked it very much. You really should consider sending them to one in your area."

Oh no. Not another whining discussion about priorities and bar mitzvahs. "I told you, Sara, not to impose your ideas. *We'll* make the decisions here, all right?"

"As you wish, Joan. All I'm saying is that these children are going to have an identity problem. Not to mention a problem of Values."

My elbow was killing me and Gil seemed to be getting heavier. "They don't need a rabbi to tell them who they are. They won't have a problem as long as they know they're loved."

"You're a funny girl, Joan," my mother-in-law sighed. "Piano lessons they can take. But Hebrew? Tsch, tsch. What priorities."

"Get off the phone," Gil whispered.

"Shall I speak to the children?" I coughed into the mouthpiece, disguising a laugh. I bit into Gil's leg in an effort to control the urge.

"Hey!" he grunted, before retaliating in kind.

"George is taking John and Laura for a walk," Sara said. "Is something wrong? You coughed. You have a cold. You should doctor yourself. Drink a lot of juice."

"I don't have a cold."

"You sound a little funny. Do you have guests? I thought I heard voices."

"No, there's no one here. I've got the TV on."

"All right. I just wanted to say hello and tell you that Stuart said he'll pick the children up tomorrow on the way home. Around one o'clock."

"Okay. Give my love. goodbye."

"Goodbye, darling."

I put the receiver back in its cradle and laughed, a little frantically.

Aside from our few actual meetings, Gil and I spoke on the phone and corresponded by mail. He wrote cryptic notes which I received at the real estate agency. These missives forced me to study the beginner's book on astronomy Gil assigned me, and would thwart Gloria's or Harrison's understanding if either should fail to heed the warning of PERSONAL printed across the envelopes. An example of such a note, finally stored under my bras and panty-hose:

Dear M42,
Ursa Major was the apex thus far. Shortly, however, all Kneels to plan and prophesy. Afterwards, we will be Sirious.

M31

Interpretation, after a struggle:

M42 is the Catalogue Number of the Great Nebula in Orion, the constellation overhead in February, the month of my birth.

Ursa Major as "the apex" refers, I suppose, to our hedonistic delights in May, but the sentence after refers to Hercules (the Kneeler), and Gil's express desire to speak of our future when he is directly overhead, in August. Sirius is night's brightest star, and indicates both the promise of a bright future and our intentions to plan for it in all earnestness by the end of the summer.

M31 is a galaxy a bit larger than ours, and looks like a fuzzy star. It is the furthest object in space that can be seen with the naked eye. It appears overhead in December, the month of Gil's birth.

There being no need to be oblique, since I addressed my letters to his apartment, my response to the above was clear and concise: Dear Gil, Up your Cassiopeia. Love, Joan. The son-of-a-bitch stepped up the pace and complexity of his letters after that, and I was required to gain at least a superficial knowledge of such matters as librations, albedo, the photosphere and Kepler's Laws of Planetary Motion, One through Three, in order to make any sense out of his communications. I was playing happy school games again.

During the weeks in which I began my study of astronomy, I also began making preliminary sketches of paintings. I'd drive to the beach with pad and pencils, and walk along the sand until I found a nice spot, sheltered near the dunes, where I'd dig in for an hour or two and draw what came to mind—whimsical creatures cavorting on a dune or along a jetty; lovers arching, Chagall-like, suspended over a tennis court; cubistic studies of sea and sail, shell or brain sectioned to reveal delicate convolutions; soft-penciled abstrations of no relevance; gross, free-flowing expression of moods.

My brief but chronic periods of shapleless depression disappeared. Although I wasn't sure of where exactly I was heading, I no longer feared the dullness of stasis or depletion. My faith in the process of becoming was restored, as my genital vitality had been born. My lifeline, from wit to clit, was secured.

Sue came with me to the beach once. We parked my car at the Marlin and walked east along Dune Road, the strip running between the ocean and the bay and bordered on either side by cozy boxes and geometric extravaganzas, unified by the land's flatness and by the way their wooden structures, however humble or lavish, reacted to salt and seasonal violence.

We saw the builders along the ocean front cutting into the already shrinking dunes with another sprawling, starkly dull condominium complex, and some others nearby, with yet another private flight of fancy. The architectural whimsies were becoming noticeably stock. The unique slope of an asymmetrical roof was repeated three houses down, only in reverse; the skylight dome, once a seemingly singular brainchild, had been procreated in multiples.

The sea air, as always, was fresh and invigorating, therapeutic. I took a deep breath.

Sue and I turned towards the beach and, walking between two weather-worn family retreats, The Lornes and Smith's Haven, slowly plodded through the sand to the ocean front.

"Okay here?" I asked, already dropping my packages of art supplies and corned beef sandwiches in what I thought was as pleasant a place as any—warm and dry, and ten yards from the tide's limit. A gull, surveying the seascape nearby, flew off as I spread my beach towel.

Susan plunked herself down in the sand and mechanically removed her sneakers and socks. "I should have gone shopping. I have nothing in the refrigerator."

"You'll go later."

"Maybe. What have you got in your pad? Let me see." She flipped through it, smiling vaguely. "Interesting. Why don't you get some things together for the sidewalk show this year?"

I had thought about grabbing a spot in the Main Street line-up this July, but the thought had never jelled. For one thing, I didn't know if I wanted to sit in a folding chair and hawk my wares, however passively, for an entire weekend. For another, I didn't have, and didn't feel like developing, a gimmick. Although the show itself is eclectic, running the gamut from Klever Kards to oriental washes, the individual display is not. Each participant has a trademark, either in subject matter or medium or style (e.g., the little lady who paints on glass, the burly man who expresses himself with nuts and bolts, the girl who paints only animals, the boy who applies oils in globs).

"I don't know if I'd fit in," I said. "I might not have enough finished stuff. I'm thinking about it, though. Hey, we missed you at the bubble Tuesday. Your substitute was lousy."

"I had an interview with a lawyer—Millbanks. Says Stuart gave him my name."

"How did it go?"

"He wants someone part time."

"Great."

"Oh, I don't know. It would mean hiring a baby sitter. Thank Stuart for me, anyway."

"You're just going to let things ride?"

"Look, my purpose was to create a new image so Roger wouldn't take me for granted. I think it just might backfire on me. He's downright hostile to the idea. I don't know how I feel any more. Now I'm kind of angry with him for demanding that I stay put. Who knows, I just might start working for spite."

"Oh, I'd love to talk to him."

"I don't think he'd love to talk to *you*." A small bitter smile darkened her face. "I think he blames you for what he calls my restlessness."

"Well, not that I mind, *am* I?"

She lay back in the sand, folding her arms under her head. "I can't blame you for his fooling around, can I? At least the Ellen Webster thing is over. I guess I'm safe. For now." She dug her heels into the sand. "Do I blame you for anything? How can I?"

"You don't think that that job would be good? Getting out of the house might—"

"Leave me alone, Joan. Do your thing." She rolled onto her stomach. "I should have kept Bobby home from school. He was coughing again this morning. Do me a favor and hand me my book, will you?"

It was clear that she wanted to be left alone.

Sue read her book while I sketched possible ideas for paintings.

The more I struggled to define my intentions, the more rewarding the effort. The more I concentrated on particulars (where to break the horizon with a curve, how to dramatize an extended arm—palm out? palm in?—when to suggest, when detail, the contours of a belly or a boat) the more enjoyable it was. I was taxing myself. It was exciting.

I was just beginning to see beyond some pencil marks. Three dancing forms, intertwined against the horizontals of sand, sea, sky. I drew rapidly—a leg there, lower left, no, more diagonal—a good line—no, curve and broaden the heel. Separate the hands. I saw the canvas. It was at least four feet high, five feet wide, prepared in pure white, waiting. I saw the white space divided into large flat surfaces of radiant colors. Saturated with light. The sand was blazing yellow. Clean lines—in acrylic? No. Oil. Oil is more responsible to mood—the purity of color has to be cut by expression, tenderness—the design can't be cold—this head should be tilted—there—

"Did you bring the corned beef?"

Wait a minute. Is the angle right? Maybe—

"Joan?"

"What? Oh. Just a second for god's sake!"

"Forget it." Susan dropped her book and rose.

Remember to correct the angle of the head. "Sorry. I got caught up. Here—let me get the sandwiches. Sure I brought the corned beef."

"Never mind. I'm not very hungry, anyway." She reached into her blue canvas bag and drew forth a wine bottle and two plastic cups. "Want some? Or are you too . . . involved?"

She made me feel guilty. "If you think you're making me feel guilty, forget it. Yeah, I'll have some wine. And you're going to have some of my corned beef if I have to stuff it down your throat." I smiled and touched her shoulder to close the rift, but it stayed with us.

She did eat a little, after all, and drank more than what I thought would normally have been her share. There was a certain seriousness in the direct way she brought the glass to her mouth and quaffed down the wine, as if she were no longer drinking to pass the time, but rather to make the time pass. She just seemed to be drifting, a woman without a reason, a theme song.

As I was gathering up my belongings my suggestion slipped out without forethought. "Why don't you just pick yourself up and get away for a few days? I'll watch the kids."

92

Susan regarded me with a fleeting look of helplessness or indifference, I couldn't tell which. "I might take you up on that offer some time," she said, putting away her book without marking a page. "Although I think you're crazy for making it."

9

During the next few weeks I underwent my yearly redefinition. I became, like the natives of Poughkeepsie whom my classmates and I tried unsuccessfully not to feel superior to, a "townie." As distinct from a summer visitor as a Ked from a Tretorn. My tan will not be as uniform. My daytime nipples will be less close to exposure.

I will be an intruder in Gristede's. The people who serve me all year will be agreeable to me, fawning to *them*. A diaphanous beach robe will brush by me in the soup aisle. A tanned and sassy ass, brazenly bursting from confining white shorts, will swing by me near a cookie display, and I will know that the people who fix my teeth, check my cervix, cut my hair and refract my eyes will be, for this saucy consumer, good enough only in the event of rural emergency.

The locale underwent its metamorphosis with a celebration of reopenings: Intimate and leather boutiques. Clam and produce stands. Beach clubs. Tennis and yacht clubs. All hawkers of summer fun and fare came out of hibernation to greet the increased demand.

As for more personal and related happenings . . .

Scorning my fear of infection for my desire for freedom, I get fitted with an IUD and dispose of my rubber insertable along with its pearly white plastic case.

I join the Marlin Beach Club for the children's sake and hire Gloria's younger sister, Lillian, as a mother's helper. (You be good children now and listen to Aunt Lillian while Uncle Gilbert is screwing Mommy, sweetie pies!)

Painting is giving me focus and discipline. I've got a mini-studio in the basement and I'm looking forward to my corner at Gil's. The reasons for my wanting to take up painting are no longer important. It's the canvases themselves that are important now.

Stuart and I attend a fund raising cocktail party at the Hampton Yacht Club sponsored by the L.I. East Arts Council, whose dual purpose is to provide incentive to local culture and the means to host an occasional talent from the Far West, like a flautist from the New York Philharmonic. We sip Bloody Marys with several natty strangers and praise last spring's exhibit of eastern Long Island artists attended by the local school children. We peer out over the Moriches Bay and chat about the substandard quality of local dancing schools and note the dire need for instructors of stringed instruments in the high school. I get involved in a not very heated discussion with a member of the Southampton town Board regarding "cluster" housing, the preservation of land, beach erosion, bulk-heating, and welfare abuse. A woman with high cheekbones and expensive boots proffers a tray of pink and white tea sandwiches and stays with us when Stuart raises the subject of "grouper" rentals. The politician assures us that another task force is being formed, whose duty will be to put some "teeth" into an ordinance which prohibits the rental of a house to more than five unrelated people. Stuart bemoans the deterioration of the "character" of the Hamptons, and the growing rate of crime—citing the number of house break-ins as an illustration. After this party Stuart, for some reason, launches a furious barrage against New York State taxes and is unusually combative toward me for the rest of the evening.

During one of his periods of all-out "fitness" awareness, Stuart arranges a mixed doubles match between us and Roger and Susan. The sand in his ankle weights swishing with every move he makes, Stuart concentrates mostly on his form. Roger, stiff and tight-lipped, seems more highly strung than his racquet. Significant, perhaps, in our developing relationship, is the fact that Roger saves his most wicked serves for me, whereas Stuart, usually a non-sexist player, offers his kindest serves to Susan.

After our mixed doubles match, I see Susan only for the last few meetings of scheduled tennis. She plays carelessly. She refuses to talk about herself. I am concerned. But I am also a selfish bitch. I have other things on my mind. I do not pursue her.

On his official arrival, I surprise Gil with cheese and champagne. We get a little drunk the Friday afternoon he moves in and, stinking of Brie, make love, for old-time's sake, on the floor. Afterward, I help him unpack his clothes and my art supplies. The next morning, when I take Laura for her dental appointment, all magazines except *Fisherman's Weekly* are being read, so I settle into an Early American side chair and occupy myself by reliving some of the special moments with Gil from the previous afternoon. I am sitting on his face, his tongue enticing me towards orgasm, when the next thing I know, Laura is relaying the news that "The dentist says I have only one cavity even though I brush my teeth lousy." Gil's tongue retracts quickly, and I am embarrassed, as though Laura has actually witnessed him dealing with *my* tender cavity.

Mr. Harrison refuses to rent a house to a young woman who obviously can't afford the rental without a little help from her friends. After she leaves the office, he rails against groupies, loose living, open sex among young people and lack of parental guidance—once again revealing his double standards. Doesn't he know that *I* know he screws the wife of a town trustee every Tuesday afternoon? Serious swapping is all right, I surmise, as long as it is practiced as a convenient accessory to the monogamous life.

I talk a lawyer from Patchogue and his "little woman" into a quaint little year-rounder with white shingles and black shutters in the hamlet of Remsenburg, whose claim to quiet fame is its longtime provision of shelter for the late P. G. Wodehouse. I immediately dispatch my income to my savings account. I am hoarding little nuts for what might be Stuart's winter of discontent.

During the first week of Gil's vacation, we were able to spend one long, sunny day together. It was like the honeymoon I ought to have had. My appetite for sex seemed insatiable, as if a lid had been removed from a bottomless pit, its walls coming alive.

Being there in the cottage made me think, as I so often did, of that first day, that first glance. Our first look had not been at, but into each other. It had been a touching, rather than an acknowledgment, of egos. It was as if our lines of observations had met head on so that we had experienced, rather than noted, our coexistence. It was the most elemental of greetings. Our first embrace had been an extension of that initial intimacy. All that followed had heightened the feeling of mutual presence, had given it form, description, and, to satisfy the analytical side of my nature, justification.

We made love early in the morning. Then we drove to the beach, parking at the Marlin. The ocean was very cold, but we went for a dip anyway, afterwards running along the beach to warm up. We rested on a beach towel, worked on the *Times* crossword puzzle.

Arm in arm, returning to the car, I saw two women I knew from the tennis club sitting on a blanket against the dunes. They waved to me. Overcoming the urge to deny their existence, I overcompensated by leading Gil to their blanket, introduced him as a good friend of mine, and squeezed his arm to prove it. Who could suspect the propriety of such open affection?

When we got back to the cottage we made some instant coffee and shared a sandwich.

We showered, soaping each other in all our shaded places, rinsing each other with infinite care. We dried together in a giant brown and black bath sheet, and slipped into bed, refreshed and ready. How unlike my honeymoon with Stuart, a festival of inhibitions in Martha's Vineyard, during which we discovered each other's little embarrassments and encysted them for times hence. Blow jobs were out. Floors were out. Blinds were drawn and lights were out. *Now* the room and I were ablaze and inhibitions were released and swept away.

"Do you have some lotion or cream we can massage one another with?" I asked, stroking his lips with the tips of my fingers. "I feel like going over you from head to toe. And you doing it to me."

He kissed my fingers and the palm of my hand. "I'll get something."

He came back with a tube of sun block cream. "Who's first?"

"I'll do you first. On your belly." I pushed the covers from the foot of the bed. "Cold?"

"No." He stretched flat out on his stomach, legs slightly parted, feet pointing outward. He placed his arms straight out to the sides. "How's that? Do you accept American Express?"

"Our method of payment here is tit for tat, sir."

"Just shut up and let your fingers do the talking."

I squeezed some cream onto his shoulders and neck, and began rubbing it in. Behind and in his ears, down his neck, into the muscles of his shoulders, up into his arms. Then I kneaded each finger, kissing his hands as I finished with each one. Then down his back and sides, digging into his firm muscles, feeling them relax under my touch. Gently pressing up and down his spine, I reached the beautiful furry globes of his behind. I felt omnipotent as I squeezed a small portion of cream onto each fleshy half. I worked the cream into them at the same time, in circular motions outward from the center, the crevice opening with each movement. He exhaled a deep sigh. Around and around, pressing with my palms, squeezing with my fingers. I began making smaller, harder circles, staying closer to the center, pushing it open each time wider and wider as he instinctively raised his behind in response to the more forceful exercise.

And then I firmly caressed the furrow, following along the passageway down to his testicles as he raised his rear still more, bending his knees to an almost kneeling position. I stroked his genitals—but tantalizingly, lightly, holding back. "Oh, god," he groaned, as I applied a series of brief, tender squeezes to his rigid organ.

I took some more of the cream and spread some on his inner thighs and legs. I rubbed it all down his legs, and repeated on his toes what I had done to his fingers. "Turn over," I ordered, after I had kissed the soles of his feet.

He turned over and I looked down at him, my heart pounding. I forced myself to keep from impaling my body on his rod, and took some more cream from the tube. "Spread out your arms and legs and don't move," I commanded, as he was reaching up to grab me.

"Please, Joan. Take me in your mouth."

"Not yet, not yet. Not until I'm ready." I put a dab of cream on his nose and chest. He obeyed me and lay flat, arms and legs out, eyes closed, frowning with discomfort. I smoothed the frown with my fingers, spread the cream in gentle motions under his eyes and around his cheeks, over and around his lips, slightly parted. Over his neck and chest. Over his nipples in little circles. Under his arms and down along his ribs. Along the hair line on his flat belly. Over the outer and inner portions of his thighs, as he began writhing under my fingers, trying to thrust his organ at me. (I'm having such a good time, sweet prick. Just wait.)

Over his thighs and belly, avoiding the insinuating cock, straining and full. "Joan! Please!"

"Not yet. You do me first!" And with that, I lay down next to

100

him, on my belly, and placed the half empty tube on his chest. "My turn, slave."

"You bitch!" he cried. "You rotten shithead!" He sat up, catching the tube of cream with one hand, pressing down on his prick with the other.

He was very impatient and eager (how delightfully cruel I felt!), but nevertheless he tried to give me equal time. And now it was his turn to assume the role of tender sadist. Alternating between delicate and firm pressures, he massaged my neck and down my back, teasing me with fleeting strokes on the sides of my breasts—brushing by, and never touching, my nipples, which tingled in delicious protest against the sheet. Then he creamed my behind and rubbed, as I had, in circular motions, baring the rear entrance to his gaze, but not to his touch. His agile fingers avoided the furrow and its rear and front apertures, the latter of which was dripping and aching with neglect. Then, disregarding my poor behind, which thrust up at him as I groaned in misery, he massaged down my legs and feet. "All right, now. Turn over and don't complain."

I did as I was told, and turned over, raising my arms over my head, spreading my legs as far apart as they would go. The peaks of my tits strained upward, imploringly, and my clitoris stung with pain. "Put your tongue somewhere, *anywhere*—please!" But he merely dabbed some cream on my shoulders and belly and proceeded to rub it in, carefully, but narrowly, bypassing all points of misery. He massaged underneath my arms and then below my breasts, pushing them upward, leaving the nipples untended. He caressed my feet, my legs, along the inner thighs, but left the hot wet mound between them in naked agony.

But *then! Then* followed the excruciating pleasure of concession—the appeasement of prolonged pain making it all the more exquisite. Finally, after what seemed like an eternity of evasion, he smiled down at me, indicating that the game was over, and slowly encased my breasts in his hands, smothering my nipples beneath his palms. I held his hands there, luxuriating beneath this warm pressure. But, needing deeper pains eased, I soon let go of his hands to position myself for more penetrating gratifications.

He sat on the bed at a slight angle, leaning back against the wall, legs akimbo, looking devilishly passive, encouraging.

I maneuvered myself into an attitude resembling a headstand, so that my face became buried in his groin, and his face confronted my own aching center. (Try and avoid that hot path now!)

He clasped me to him, bracing my inverted body against him. A grunt of satisfaction escaped his lips as he sank them into my fissure, sucking and biting with abandoned vigor at that taut nub protruding from the jelly. I, in turn, opened my mouth wide and filled it with as much of his gloriously huge prick as I could, sucking at it like a giant straw.

How he ravaged that tender mound—the pain of longing and the promise of pleasure concentrated in that small pellet exposed to the wanton pressures of lips and teeth. And then tongue, licking and pressing it and the surrounding flesh, while hands moved over my back and down into the damp furrow. Fingers rubbed, stretched, kneaded the rear entrance until the muscles gave in, allowing them to probe within. They bore into the opening, bluntly and mercilessly broadening that channel, while the tongue penetrated the easier, softer entrance. The tongue writhed like a snake inside its pit and I cried out as its prey yielded, setting off a wave of spasms. This series of contractions and dilations—almost unbearable, it was so intensely titillating —sparked the undulations which traveled deeper and deeper into my belly, reverberating through my body, ending in my limbs, hands, feet, tingling and weakened by the echos of savage pleasure.

Instinctively, I clamped down on my mouthful, which exploded into my throat. Sap surging into the gullet, ingested, leaving a pocket of cream in the cheek. Oozing out of the mouth. Consummation, tasted and sustained by deep breaths and deeper sounds.

We sank to the sheets.

He whispered into the burning bush. "I love you."

I was quietly crying against his gummy thigh those tears of joy that had never dropped in Martha's Vineyard. Thank you, thank you. "Oh, sweetheart."

"Do you love me?" he asked, barely audible.

"Yes."

"*Say* it then."

"I love you."

"Only me?"

Oh, sweet baby from another time, another world—*my* dumb-ass world. "Only you."

"I don't know if I believe you."

"Don't spoil it, Gil."

"Are you going to tell your husband about us, then?"

"I said I would."

"When?"

"Sweetheart—don't be a nag. I love you."

"When?"

The urgency was badly timed. We should be relaxing now, floating free. "Remember the bright star, Sirius, in our letters. We said August."

"Tell him sooner."

I wanted to.

Only two weeks after I set up my easel in Gil's cottage, I felt as though it had always been there. The familiar smell of drying oils which greeted me as I opened the door promised work and love. Some of the best moments had found me simultaneously on the brink of artistic success and physical embrace.

"It's good to be home," I said, entering. I dropped my bag where I stood and Gil and I kissed.

"It's a beautiful morning," he said.

"Again."

"Let's take off today and head out east, maybe to Montauk."

"That sounds good." I surveyed the canvas I had been working on and knew exactly where I would have begun painting that day. The subject was a man embracing a child and it wasn't working. "I'll pack a lunch."

"It's already packed," Gil said, gesturing towards the kitchen area.

"You know, that guy's foot is going to bug me all day," I said, looking back at the canvas.

"Try to put him out of your mind, sweetheart," he cajoled, turning my face towards his.

"I think I probably can manage that," I answered, wondering if I really could.

As we were driving east towards the end of the Island and comfortable anonymity, I thought about that course at C. W. Post I had been debating about. "I'm going to take it," I decided.

"What are you going to take, hon?"

"That class I had mentioned to you. Four hours a week in August. It's practical instruction on media and design, and I could use it."

"Why? I think your stuff is great."

I caressed his thigh. "I see you don't have the same perfectionist standards for my work as for yours. Don't forget, I've seen you spend an entire day refining one page of dazzling brilliance."

He covered my hand with his. "That's because I'm less of a natural at what I do."

"Bull. It's because you consider yourself a professional and me a dabbler."

"Don't be an ass. I'm just jealous of the time you spend away from me."

"A few hours a week? Come on. You want my painting to be forever a secondary—*domestic* sort of thing." I pinched his thigh. "Don't you, you son of a bitch?"

"Oh, take the course, for god's sake. See if I care," he returned, with just a hint of malice in the jesting tone.

"How cavalier of you," I sighed. "Thank you, daddy."

"You're too much. Find an apple for me, will you?" he said, changing the subject, none too soon.

Whatever hazards there were in our arrangement, they were absorbed by the sun, and also by willpower.

Stripped down to our bathing suits, we spent a lovely time

walking along the shore and talking about our future together. We had the beach practically to ourselves. We populated the clean stretch of sand with our fancies. We imagined scenes of magnificent banality, like the two of us sitting on our living room floor doing the *Times* crossword, while our chicken roasted in the oven. We conjured up scenes of sociability—a cocktail party, for instance, where the casualness of our friends' conversation acknowledged our legitimacy as a couple.

After we ate our sandwiches and drank our wine we lay back together, side by side, letting the sun soak into us. My eyes were closed and my perceptions eddied out from around our clasped hands, our only contact with each other. That gentle pressure inspired loving fantasies that formed and dissolved and formed again, like waves. I felt passive, warm, content. I had just begun to fashion my own life, but what a temptation it was to yield myself to my sculptor's beautiful and tender hands. Independence tugged at my heartstrings and curiosity beckoned invention, but at that moment in the sun I might have granted him absolute power over my will, snuggling up under the protective mantle of love from a compassionate monarch.

The occasional sound of gulls, usually raucous, soothed me. I was almost drawn into sleep when Gil broke the spell by blocking out the sun.

I opened my eyes. He was leaning over me, his face close to mine. There was a small patch of sand under his ear and I brushed it away. "Hi," he whispered. "What are you thinking about?" He lay his head on my shoulder and rested his body against mine.

Stroking his strong back, flecked with sand, and breathing in the odor of his perspiration, I was summoned back to the realm of experience.

Reality was more gritty, more exciting than the floating constructs of dreams. "I wasn't really *thinking* about anything. I was seeing. You just popped in on a beautiful picture. We were lying naked on our backs, side by side. A naked infant was crawling all over us. It was very sweet."

He paused, and then, "I don't like the idea of your having had that kind of feeling with someone else. But of course you know that."

"But I never *had* that feeling with anyone else."

Oddly enough, the truth was a revelation to me.

I ran my finger over the contours of his ear. I said, "This little thing was crawling over us, grabbing us with his tiny fingers, drooling on us, pulling at our hair. We tried to lie still, but he tickled us with his random movements. What he did was illuminate the love I now seem to have for my own—for our—body."

"Was he *our* baby? Or yours?"

"I had no feeling of ownership. The baby was an emanation of our love." Each thought was a discovery. "You know, just the possibility of our enjoying a baby of our own is as definitive as the real thing. It describes real emotions. It sounds peculiar, I know, but it's a new kind of love for me."

Never having experienced the feeling of oneness with Stuart, the pleasure derived from our children was never really shared. Our pleasures had at times abutted, never merged.

Now, without his knowing it, Gil eased into my organic family, becoming a member not by decree, but by nature. He pressed his face against my neck and held me very tightly. Soon, I knew, dusk would come and we would be on our way back to the demands of custom and of our separate minds. But if time should ever negate our mutual resolve, this day in the sun had shown me something about my affections that could never be refuted.

10

I had been painting, swimming, playing an occasional match, and generally neglecting my children when, on a Wednesday morning in the middle of July, I received the invitation that Dusty Bantom had promised and I'd forgotten about.

"We're having a few new and old friends over Saturday evening. It will be *very* informal," she stipulated. "As always. I hope you and your husband will be able to come."

Stuart was going to be in Philadelphia taking a four-day seminar on the Tax Structure of the Professional Corporation, but I didn't see why the Liberty Bell couldn't ring for *me.*

"I'm afraid my husband will be out of town," I said, hoping she would take the initiative and ask me to drop by, anyway.

"That's too bad. But do come yourself, dear—with or without an escort."

"Well—"

"And come in tennis togs if you like. If it's a pleasant evening I'm sure some of our group will want to play."

"I'd love to."

"Bring a bathing suit, too, if the mood strikes. See you about six or so. There'll be plenty of food and drink. And, oh yes, I wonder if you'd reach the Clarks for me. We adore the house, but there's something gone awry with the plumbing in the upstairs bathrooms."

"I'll have them send someone over for you."

"You're a dear. Looking forward to seeing you."

I wanted to go to the party with Gil. I had enjoyed seeing him in the company of others. A few days ago three of his students had visited him, staying overnight in sleeping bags on the floor. I spent the afternoon with them. Gil was so natural with the young men, falling into the role of brotherly mentor so easily. I was envious of them. I wished I could convince Gil that I was just as loyal to him as they were. I couldn't help it if I was married when he found me.

Later that day, when he was stooped over his footnotes and I was stretching a canvas, I mentioned the Bantom's party. "Want to go?" I asked. "I'm in the mood for a bash."

He marked a spot on the paper and turned toward me. "But darling, that's the weekend my sister is coming in from Cincinnati. Remember—the one who couldn't make Lincoln Center?" The sparkle shown through his glasses.

I smoothed the canvas. "Shall we see her together?"

"She's in the process of getting a divorce, due for a cry with shoulder included. It's my turn to comfort big sister. It's always been the other way around. I think I better see her alone."

"Oh . . . Stuart will be in Philadelphia. Maybe I'll go myself, then."

Gil half rose from the chair, bumping his hip on the table. "Alone?"

"Yes."

"Don't." He had risen from his chair to confront me.

"Why not?"

"I don't like the idea of your appearing to be on the make. Or are you?" Was he looking stern or suspicious?

"How can you say that?"

"Do I really know you, Joan?"

"Better than anybody."

"That might not be good enough—if it's true. How can I be sure of your motivations?"

"Try faith," I said.

"I lose it when I see you want to have yourself a god damn ball without me."

"I guess some people need more time than others to test the faith of their convictions. It looks like you're one of them."

He laughed sardonically. "There's another good one. And how much time do you need before you tell the husband you're getting out?"

"Listening to you now? More than I thought."

"Oh? Maybe you just need time to play the field, see if you can do better." More bitterly, "How the hell do I know you haven't been screwing around all along?"

I had been flattered by Gil's possessiveness. Now it grated, angered me. His love made me whole. His distrust was a call to arms.

"You go a little too far," I said.

"You'll be *going* to this party, then?"

"Yes."

The Bantoms were camping out in one of Quogue's white-columned mansions—surrounded, protected, and adorned by an array of magnificent pines and hemlocks. A black wrought-iron gate swinging ajar between two brick pillars marked the entrance of the three acre estate and the name of its summer residents was appended near its foot in letters of modest roman.

I parked my VW on the side of the road near the entrance, right behind an old Ferrari, and took a final look at myself in the visor mirror. I fluffed up my hair and slid out the door, grabbing my newly strung Head Competition and my canvas shoulder bag. I was wearing a white knit tennis dress and a cardigan. Feeling insecure, generally apprehensive, and lost without Gil whom I hadn't seen since our standoff, I dared myself to feel confident. Well educated, well toned, uncommitted and on my own! I almost managed to deceive myself.

When I arrived, the party had been in progress long enough for small sipping and chatting cliques to have been formed. Some of the thirty or forty guests were scattered around the romanesque pool, sitting or posing about the large brick patio, claiming hors d'ouevres proffered by two young girls with trays. Others sat or moved about in the connecting glass-enclosed room. A recent addition to the old house, it was done in the style of cushioned contemporary. The bartender was busily mixing drinks in a popular corner of the room.

The clay tennis court, some sixty yards from the pool area, was swept clean and smooth, ready for its first combatants. A few of the guests were dressed for the game.

As Dusty approached me on the patio, I noticed she was limping slightly. Still, she looked lovely in her long velour wrap. I lay down my racquet and bag. She clasped my hands with the gentle pressure of a dear, dear friend. "So glad you could come—and prepared to *play!*" She raised the wrap and pointed to her ankle, bound in an elastic bandage. "Sprained it on the court yesterday," she sighed. She introduced me to a few people as she led me to the bar, and then left me to my own devices.

It was easier after a drink.

I drifted and mingled, the fingers of my right hand becoming numb from the ice in my glass.

A tall, slightly stooped gentleman was speaking to Bill Bantom.

"... already sold a few to the Museum of Modern Art. The lad's going places, I can tell you. Just the kind of abstract purism Dusty goes for. You'll have to come by and—"

A jaunty, untidy young man interrupted. "Say, if it isn't the old mode merchant! How are you doing?" he smiled, extending his hand. "What's the new style this season?"

Bill introduced me to the East Side art dealer and the West Village artist.

"Do you paint, carve, or—batique, Joan?" the artist asked me.

"I paint."

"You gotta watch out for these guys," he muttered, as a clearly audible aside. "They seduce souls." He laughed uncomfortably. I wondered if his churlish independence was his way of sucking up. I took a healthy gulp of my Bloody Mary and moved on.

Two groomed and garnished ladies were chatting together.

"Were you in town today? It was positively teeming with all the lean and hungry singles. I've never seen so many nose jobs in my life."

"Quiet desperation is so much more civilized, don't you agree?" A fragile laugh.

"It makes me seriously consider becoming a recluse!"

"I'm sure. Didn't I see you at Clara's last week?"

"Wasn't that an extravaganza!"

"Did you meet anyone?"

"A darling widower. I've got him with me now." She inclined her head. "See? There, in the brown shirt? I'd better take more of an interest. Excuse me."

"Aah, but I must be introduced!"

They headed for him together, fingers checking for stray hairs and other loose ends.

Gil must be seeing his sister now, I thought. I wondered what she was like.

An oriental photographer with a Nikon and assorted lenses dangling from his body arrived in the company of a ravishing Black beauty, and a pale, but gloriously fit-looking young man, who walked in the manner of a steely-spined duck and who must certainly be a dancer. Of course. James Lynn of the Metropolitan Ballet Company. I had seen his face with opera glasses from a ring at the State Theatre.

"You must be James Lynn," I said, entering the group, shifting my drink to my left hand.

"Yes," he said, pleased that I had recognized him. He had a strong handshake.

"My kids and I saw you in *Coppelia*," I said, suddenly feeling like a fool. "You were a charming Franz."

Mr. Lynn relaxed into third position. "Thanks. And you're . . . ?"

"Joan. Joan Hiller."

He introduced me to the photographer, Son Kim, and the milk chocolate beauty, Zenia, his model. Everything about her was extravagant. Her hair, long and untamed. Her body, tall and supple. She exuded warmth. I learned that she was the heroine of Son Kim's book, *Sappho in the Hamptons,* replete, I imagined, with ardent shots on the dunes.

Zenia tousled James's blond hair affectionately. "Jimmy's writing a screenplay."

The dancer shifted from third position to second, and back again.

"How nice," I said.

"It's about a dancer's battle with leukemia," Zenia said. "Nothing personal," she added.

I drained my Bloody Mary.

"Little quiches," a waitress explained, as I looked questioning at her tray. I took one.

"Let me get you another drink," Son Kim said, taking the glass from my hand. "A Bloody Mary, wasn't it?"

The drink Mr. Kim returned with was very strong. "So . . . adolable!" cooed Zenia, pinching his round cheeks. I winced.

As much as I tried to exclude Gil from this party, his sharply drawn image kept intruding on the scene. I drank my Bloody Mary if only to blur the picture.

The Bantoms' Park Avenue internist, a man full of gusto, was explaining the effects of amylnitrate to a group of intent listeners. "It's a drug used for dilating coronary arteries for patients with angina pectoris. But those are not the *only* vessels they affect!"

"I don't give him a chance to get in much golf on Wednesdays," chortled the buoyant woman to his left.

"You look awfully familiar," I said to a tipsy little man tapping a swizzle stick against the rim of his glass.

"I'll give you three guesses. You win a trip to Las Vegas if you get it in one."

The large woman with him shook her head. "No more quizzes," she sighed. From his frown I guessed she was his wife. Had she given away a clue?

"You're on a game show, maybe?"

"You're as far as Cleveland," he said.

"I give up."

"Everybody's got one."

"One what?"

"That's the name of the show, babe! Clint West? Host?"

"Sorry. One of my kids must have had it on and I . . . I don't usually watch game—"

"That's okay. Win some, lose some." He teetered. "Excuse me, gals. Got to find the little boys' room. Keep out of trouble, now!" He flashed us a capped smile.

I hurt. Surfacing so quickly after being with Gil was giving me the bends.

A woman with a foreign accent and big hoop earrings held my wrist. I could see the remnants of oil paint under her nails. "But how *fortunate* you are to live out here all year, Joan—it's Joan, isn't it, yes? I myself am a prisoner of concrete and steel, but if you cut out my soul—"

"Your refill, m'am? A Tom Collins?"

The sparkling lady took her drink and nodded appreciation. "—my soul, yes?—if you cut it out from me you would find in it stretches of dune, diving gulls, perhaps even a storm at sea, yes? You are so lucky, my dear!" She waved frantically to someone across the pool. "Robert, my love! It's been *months!*" A few yards away, Son Kim snapped her picture as she took flight.

The architect was tall, spare and spirited, a female Don Quixote. "When I think of the Hamptons, I think of Utzon's glorious mixed metaphor."

"Who?"

"Utzon—the designer of the Sydney Opera House."

"Oh, yes," I said, with an agreeable nod of my head, pretending to know. Condemning myself as a phony, I took another sip of my drink and helped myself to a canape from the tray poised temporarily at my elbow.

"Such a magnificent union of function and beauty!" the architect continued.

I drifted in and out of groups, overhearing fragments of conversation and trying to react appropriately. Here, with a look of interest; there, with an appreciative laugh. It was as if I were acting a bit part in a play I hadn't read. I didn't feel comfortable on this stage.

"The difference is whereas Bill invests in the creative and performing arts, Dusty patronizes them."

". . . so, sex is a fact of nature that brings people together, and marriage is an institution that holds society together and draws people apart."

"Jesus, Helen, I only asked if he was a good lay."

"No, I don't care to live in a precious enclave of *artistes,* thank you. Give up my little cell in the stinking melting pot? Not on your life!"

"Have you seen that girl in the health food store? Hell, she charmed me into buying a bottle of B-14, mineral supplements, and a can of the most rotten tasting powder."

"Any results?"

"My tennis elbow has taken on a healthy glow."

"Making *Death of a Salesman* into a *musical comedy?* No!"

"Yes!"

Guests were wandering off, to other parties, other places. Clint West, host of the game show, was approaching me with his big-headed Prince. Would I have the heart to say no?

"Wife's asleep. Care to take out your aggressions on the court with me?" he asked.

"I don't know how steady a partner I'd be," I answered, backing away from his sobering breath.

"You can't fool me, young lady. You know the score!"

I surrendered. "All right. I hope we'll be able to get the court."

"Oh yes," he leered, listing a bit from his alcohol overload. "We're sure to get a piece of the action." Wink, wink. His poor wife.

I took off my cardigan and got my racquet and together we walked over to the court.

Millicent, the wiry architect, and Philip, a professor from Easthampton, were battling out a game of singles. "What's the score here?" Clint called, distracting the players in the middle of a point.

"*Now* it's four serving five!" said Millicent, who had just looked up and missed an easy forehand. "Your serve, Philip!"

"Take the point over," her opponent called.

"Come on, now, let's not be party poopers," my quick-witted companion objected. "Let's play some *doubles* here!" He turned his glassy eyes to me and leaned into the side of my body. "We challenge you guys, don't we?"

"I suppose so," I answered feebly.

Philip, an agreeable man, raised his slender hands apologetically. "Say, we've been playing for a while. Why don't you two play singles?"

But Clint, a game show person by nature as well as profession, was determined to set up the rules. He noticed that a few more people were sauntering towards the court, racquets and drinks in hand, laughing together. "No, no. Doubles will be more fun. We'll play, let me see, first to reach seven points—tie-breakers—lots of excitement!"

They agreed. Millicent retied her laces, and Philip joined her on her side of the court.

We warmed up for a few minutes and I could see that my leprechaun was going to be a challenge to me. He swayed and stumbled once during our practice period, and helped himself to a swig of someone's drink before Millicent spun her racquet to determine first server. "Up or down?" she called.

"Give it a chance!" Clint snickered.

"C'mon. We'll take up," I said.

It was up, and Clint elected to serve first.

"Right in!" he called, refraining from taking a few practice serves. I was standing at the baseline. I didn't know whether to cover the net or defensively keep back in the event of a hard return of a weak serve. I had no time to decide.

Up went the ball. Wham! Into the net. Up again. Plop. An impotent second serve. Bam! Millicent, tasting blood, hauled off and hit one over the fence. "Damn!" she mumbled.

"Let's keep a lid on," Clint snickered, jumping up and down, preparing himself for the second point. Up it went. Down it came, skidding off the tape at a lucky angle. "Oh, dear!" exclaimed Millicent, as she watched the ball sail past her partner.

Their luck turned when Philip served. I was playing backhand and was receiving his second service after Clint had blown the first on a hard ball served to his feet. Philip, an awkward but hard server, tossed the ball and whacked it. It hurtled towards my forehand and in defending myself I inadvertently hit it right to Millicent's racquet. She attempted a lob, which failed; but Clint attempted an easy overhead, which failed even worse—he smashed it into the net and almost fell over.

It was my turn to serve. I took the two traditional practice shots, and tried a fast-paced serve down the line to Philip's backhand. He endeavored to ram it down my man's throat, but it angled out of the court, saving both my point and Clint's life.

Millicent returned my serve to my forehand and I tried a drop shot return to her backhand, forcing her to race to the net. Unfortunately, the ball spun towards her when it bounced and she was able to meet it, breathing hard. Surprised, I received the ball and essayed a last minute cross court past Philip. He was on it, however, and succeeded where I had failed.

The score was three, three.

Millicent served to Clint. The ball ricocheted off his racquet handle and accidentally landed as a winning shot across the court.

I mopped my sweaty brow with my wrist band and crouched at the baseline, zeroing in on the game. While my other senses were rather slushy, my court sense at least *seemed* acute, making up in inner space what I lacked in actual awareness. I felt the map of the court in my bones.

Millicent served to me. I hit a hard top-spin down the middle. Philip surprised me with an ungraceful but successful lunge and Clint was suddenly faced with a ball down *his* middle.

"Sorry!" said Philip. "Are you hurt? It was purely a reflex shot!"

"No harm done!" said Clint. He was having a great time.

We lost four to seven, in spite of a few long rallies, my forte, and Clint prepared to leap over the net in a gesture of suicidal merriment. At the last moment, however, he turned his head towards me and saw me fanning my damp legs with my skirt. This must have tripped the game buzzer in his head. He stopped dead in his tracks.

"Hey!" he exclaimed, dropping his racquet. "Have I got a terrific idea here!" With that, he lifted his shirt over his head and tossed it aside. "Losers have to take something off. Let's go, Joan!"

"I don't know," I said.

"Sounds like a great way to relax," offered James, the dancer, from the sidelines. "Come on, Joan. Release the inner spirit!" The photographer, Son Kim, and Zenia were nodding their approval.

"May I borrow a racquet, Dusty?" James asked. "I'd like to try my hand at this. I'll play barefoot."

"Why, of course," said Dusty, admiring his thighs. "Bill, dear? Will you run and fetch the racquets?"

The Bloody Marys had dulled my ability to appraise the situation, and the exercise of tennis had engaged me in it.

As a loser of the match I removed my sneakers.

James took off his sandals and went through a series of knee bends. Bill brought him two racquets and he chose the more comfortable one. "Now, all I have to do is hit the ball with this thing," he said. He vaulted over the net like a cossack.

James was warmed up, and now he was thirsty. He suggested that Clint get some drinks for us while he and his partner, Zenia, played the winners, Millicent and Philip. "The bartender's gone, and so's everyone else but us," he said. "You can check up on your wife while you're at it. And bring some ice, okay?"

Clint went weaving off. I went to help him, as Zenia stepped onto the court to explain the essentials of the game to her partner.

Clint's wife awoke for a moment. "What are you going?" she yawned.

"Playing tennis," Clint replied.

"I really should learn the game," she crooned, and fell back to sleep.

We returned, with glasses, ice, and bottles, just as the game was about to begin. I sat down in the grass and poured myself a drink. Clint sat by my side, bare-chested and reeling, and tried to embrace me, but my attentions were divided between James and Zenia.

During this unusual match the spirit of the voyeur dominated Philip's game (he played with incredible accuracy and strength), and the spirit of the exhibitionist dominated the model's (she held back whatever strengths, if any, she had). It was clear that she wanted to take something off and that he wanted to see her do it.

James danced around the court, occasionally hitting the ball. His main purpose was evidently to exhibit his physical grace.

Zenia was the third server, sumptuous, powerless. Her serve, like the rest of her game, was shallow and ineffective. Son Kim, maneuvering around the periphery of the court, his camera clicking away, asked her to take her serve over. "On your toes!" he called. "Get the tossing arm higher! Back further with the racquet arm! Good! Good! Stick the tongue between the lips! Concentrate! A little frown, please! So!" Click. Click. The pink shirt was lifted, exposing a bit of midriff. All eyes were on it. "So!" Click. Click. The ball was finally thrown. I envisioned another hot seller, *Sappho Plays Tennis,* perhaps?

Son Kim frequently interrupted the game until its foregone conclusion. At that historic moment, the compassionate girl kindly chose to remove her pink shirt, showing us how reality can sometimes top the imagination.

How splendid were those carob-tipped cocoa globes, now freed from their confines, and how our bleary eyes devoured their surprise feast!

James, following the rules, took off his tennis shirt and revealed an admirable chest.

Near me, Clint fidgeted. Dusty sat on the sidelines, on Clint's discarded shirt and Bill stood close to her, nursing his drink. "Why don't you join the game, dear," she suggested, massaging her ankle.

"Does anybody mind if I play again?" Zenia asked.

"Not at all," said Philip cheerfully. "Millicent and I will take time out."

"Ah, but I want to play again!" objected Millicent energetically. "This is a tremendous outlet for me! Does anyone have a drink for me?"

"I'll play with you, Millie," offered Bill. "Let's go."

"Where's my drink?"

Dusty poured her one. Millicent belted most of it down. Son Kim finished it.

And now the photographer was ready. The players took their places. Nobody thought of asking Bill if he wanted to warm up.

Zenia was receiving his serve. She crouched into position. The angle of her breasts changed. Click. Bill sent the ball over the net. Out. He tried again, but in mid-toss Mr. Kim called an order to Zenia—"Bend lower. Let us see the panties, please!"—and Bill lost whatever concentration he had mustered. He hit the ball into the net.

But Zenia, sweet pea that she was, called to him in her breathy high-pitched voice, "Take two!" and immediately Clint, court jester, jumped up and ran to her side. "Thanks, don't mind if I do!" he exclaimed, eagerly grabbing both her darling tits with his forceful little hands. Son Kim began flinging what I assumed to be Korean curses at him.

Zenia sprang away from her assailant and clutched at herself protectively. I jumped to her rescue and, with her partner, dragged Clint away, clawing at the air.

The game was begun again, Bill winning one and losing one of

119

his service points. The model served next and was a delight to behold. Clint steadied himself by hanging onto my arm. Onlookers gasped when she won both her give-away points by unintentionally distracting her opponents, and groaned when Millicent tried to hit one down the line and hit it into the net instead. The score was three to one in favor of Zenia, when Millicent and Bill made an all-out effort to win. Zenia tried to make it easy for them by missing anything that came her way. Bill, however, had some athletic pride. "Keep your alley covered, Z," he admonished.

"No!" whined Clint. "Give us a look at it!" Bill refused to play the fool. With a few well placed drop shots and one dilly of a smash (Millicent was herself too smashed to do much in the way of defense), he won the game and our disfavor at the same time.

Gallantly, the losers took off some of their clothing. Philip exposed his grey-haired chest. Millicent removed her dress and brassiere ("Double fault," Clint muttered), winning the hearts, if not the less noble organs, of her audience.

Clint and I played the winners, Philip and Millicent. Unable to answer Bill's strength with an impressive counterattack, we lost the match, and I, my socks.

Before long Zenia lost another round and another article of clothing. Delicately, she reached under her skirt and looped her thumbs under the elastic waistband of her pink tennis panties.

Very slowly, as if it took some effort, she pulled them down, bending a little so that a bit of the cleft tantalized those of us lucky enough to be positioned directly behind her. She turned in the middle of her act, in order to reangle herself for her photographer, and offered us different views. With careful deliberation she stepped out of the pants and cavalierly tossed them to her partner, James. She raised her arms above her head and arched her back, stretching her oh so tired muscles, incidentally exposing the ebony triangle that had been hidden by her skirt.

The court lights created a kind of strobe light phenomenon, cancelling out the world beyond their range.

The game continued.

By arguing over a technicality, we reminded ourselves that we were only playing a game. Should Bill, for example, be permitted to change racquets when a string broke?

Were we more comfortable giving in to our baser inclinations if we viewed them as having been imposed on us from without? Pardon me while I bare my ass, folks. Just following the rules.

Pants, like the last vestige of an ethic, make all the difference. One strip of nylon against a crotch and you're safe and sound. Remove that thin strip and the universe is suddenly pressing up between your legs, all galactic energy focusing up into your folds. After another loss, I removed my own, fascinated by the publicity of the act.

At last, Dusty rose to her feet. "All right," she said. "Someone give me a racquet. I'm going to play on this ankle!" She threw off her sandals. "I want to play some tennis!"

"But Dusty," objected Bill, "you'll hurt—"

"No, no!" exclaimed James. "The lady will sit on top of me and not exert one bit of pressure on her lovely little ankle! Here, let me help you take off your dress. We'll both be more comfortable."

"How kind of you." The wrap was duly removed and neatly folded and laid aside. Dusty was now clad only in a blue lace bra. "Upsy daisy!" said James, hoisting her onto his shoulders. "Someone give the lady a racquet, please!" Her husband handed her his.

"We need challengers," said Dusty from her lofty perch.

"I volunteer," chirped Zenia.

"As host, I claim the honor of assist," said Bill. He stripped.

Zenia was set astride Bill. She lifted her skirt to her waist, allowing her shimmering crotch to rest comfortably against his neck. His cock stood at attention.

The precarious group tilted onto the court, and the untraditional set was begun.

The women alternated between squeals of laughter and screams of terror as the men swayed beneath them. "A structural marvel!" Millicent sighed, studying Zenia, atop Bill.

"Watch out!" called Dusty, as James backed up for her to return a lob, almost falling over. He recovered, converting the slip into a *glissade*. He began moving about the court as though he were performing a lovely *pas de deux*. Dusty, catching on, began moving her arms and legs as if she were a ballerina.

Zenia, attempting to return a high ball, caused her partner to lose his balance. They fell, and the game was over. It had served its purpose. The ice had been broken.

After her spill, Zenia was resting in the grass. Clint, in a state of agitation, took advantage of her vulnerable position and fell upon her. Son Kim let fly his epithets as he and I rescued Zenia.

As Clint sought solace from Dusty and Bill, I watched Zenia as she began opening and closing her legs like bellows, fanning the flame of my curiosity. What would it be like to touch the tender rose flesh with the tips of my fingers? Or to taste a known but oh so foreign morsel? What would it feel like to bring this glossy dark beauty to the point of arched, groaning climax? To have that sunless chamber of sensation pulsating around my fingers or my tongue? Would there be a burning, longing pleasure in my loins? Would I feel a new and voluptuous sense of power? I wanted to be tested.

As if he had heard my thoughts, Son Kim requested my presence in the next series of arrangements. It was not my doing, then. I was merely to be a draftee in the advancement of artistic achievement!

A racquet was placed at Zenia's still sneakered feet; a single optic yellow ball, between her legs, for aesthetic balance. Instructed to strip the remainder of my clothing, then sit at her hip and look down on her lovingly, I obeyed. Then I was asked to place a hand on one of her burnished breasts, so that I would touch, but not completely obscure, the nipple. I had never touched a breast other than my own. Gingerly I lay my hand against the cool, smooth cushion. I stroked her covertly and her chest began to heave. Very pleasant.

Son Kim requested that I rest my mouth against hers. This I found disagreeable. The next shot took place between her legs, where I was to touch her glistening valley as lyrically as possible. Again captivated, bewitched by the newness of the experience.

122

Tentatively, I stroked the soft damp. It pleased Zenia. I exerted a little more pressure. It thrilled me that I knew exactly how to move my fingers against her in order to cause the reaction I sought. But I was objective. So objective. She lay there, roughly in my image, responding to my ministrations in much the same way I would under the touch, and yet I felt as neutral towards her as I would to a reflection in the mirror. I bent towards the zone of activity, looking, studying. I pushed and rubbed against the clinging pressures. Zenia reached up and pulled me closer towards what had only been an imagined experience.

The odor of feminity startled me. I was not prepared for this inhalation of myself. I could feel neutral toward the pressures on a roving finger, but an odor either tantalized or repelled. The particularity of it removed the experience from dream and replaced my curiosity with resistance. I was too close to her, to myself, between my own thighs. This magnification of self-love appalled me as did, suddenly, my nakedness. Son Kim froze another image, underlining what was already hyperbole.

"I'm sorry," I said, withdrawing from the experiment.

Zenia was distressed, frowning.

"I'm sorry," I repeated, rising, becoming apprehensive. I reached for my clothes.

Philip approached. Embracing me, he said, "Come, be with me."

The contact, another shock, recalled Gil's image. "Please," I said, extricating myself.

As I moved aside to dress, Millicent knelt beside Zenia. Philip was joining her. The others were already engaged in acts of gratification.

I watched the bodies, contorting in the light of the tennis lanterns and the moon. Somewhere in the darkness a cat whined. I might have been in the Adamite's *Garden of Delights,* the strangely erotic and disordered paradise of Hieronymous Bosch. In this irreverent Eden there was no reckoning with sin, but weird creatures hung about everywhere and a kind of extravagant unreason prevailed. I was an uneasy visitor here.

A wail filled the air.

Clint's wife had awakened and, from poolside, had just seen him in the arms of Dusty Bantom. The setting, marooned from the world beyond the tennis lanterns, was replaced on the map of Long Island by this intrusion.

The game was explained. Everything had been all in fun, one thing had led to another. How could anyone with a sense of humor and even the smattering of sophistication have taken such a frolic seriously. Couldn't she understand? Clint, who had so brazenly advanced on Zenia and so unabashedly lain with Dusty, stood before his wife, trying to shield his genitals from her view.

The party was over, but before we dispersed propriety was restored. Clothes were donned, coffee was drunk, conversation returned to such matters as the pastry Zenia turned down because she was watching her weight.

As I thanked the host and hostess for a lovely evening, I felt as if a movie had just been run backwards.

It was well past midnight when I arrived home, a tired wreck, only to discover that the sitter had been dismissed by Stuart, who had returned from Philadelphia a day early and was now lying in wait.

I was in no mood for a heart to heart.

124

11

Stuart and I were not destined for subdued conversation. He explained, curtly, that the seminar had been a repetitive drag. I mumbled something about an exhausting tennis match and crept into the bathroom to wash up.

He was just launching into a line of questioning that would require maximum creativity on my part, when the phone rang. My mouth full of toothpaste, but instinctively knowing that I should be the one to answer it, I made a noble dash for the phone. Stuart, however, only had to reach across the bed and was the one to greet the late caller with a puzzled "Hello?"

There was a pause. Stuart sat bolt upright. "What do you mean, who the hell am *I*? Who the hell are *you*?" I tried to grab the receiver away from him, my mouth full of suds, but he pushed me away. I hastened downstairs to the kitchen extension and grabbed the receiver off the hook. "Who ish dish?" I yelled, gagging on the toothpaste.

Gil's sonorous voice bellowed into my ear. "Not only do you bring home stray dogs, but you're drunk, too!"

I emptied my mouth on my tennis skirt. "You don't know what you're talking about!"

"Who's there?" Stuart yelled.

"Don't wake the kids!" I implored.

"Get that man off the phone!" Gil shouted.

"Who the hell do you think you are, telling me to get off this phone?" demanded Stuart.

"Gil," I said, "wait a min—"

"I won't talk to you until that bastard gets off the line!"

"Who are you calling a bastard?" cried Stuart.

"You, you son-of-a-bitch! Hang up!"

"Stop Gil! It's—"

"You going to tell me this is a party line? Get him off! Don't I at least have priority over a one-night stand?"

"I'm the *husband* around here!" Stuart barked. "Who is this?"

"Bullshit! The husband is in Philadelphia!"

"Not any more he isn't!"

"He's telling the truth," I wailed. "Stop!"

"You keep out of this," Stuart snarled. "Now, who the hell *are* you?"

"If you're talking about me, I'm the love of her life—except on Saturdays. Didn't she tell you? Must have slipped her mind!"

"Is this some kind of hoax?" Stuart hissed into the receiver. "Is this a trick?"

"Yes, yes it is!" I answered. "Hang up for god's sake. Don't encourage it!"

"Stay where you are, C.P.A.! There's an amoeba shaped freckle on her left cheek. Am I lying?"

The puzzled anger was relayed right through the wire. "I . . . But there *are* no freckles on her face."

"On her ass, chump. On her *ass!*"

"Just a minute!" There was a scurrying of footsteps. Stuart was after me.

I screamed into the receiver "This was not the way it was supposed to happen!" when Stuart was on me, tearing at my pants. "Oh, for Chrissake," I groaned. "Don't bother to look. It's there."

Stuart was standing over me, controlling himself.

126

Trying not to raise my voice, "Why did you do this?" I enunciated into the receiver.

"What's the difference. You were *never* going to tell him you belong to me! Top hit for the summer, and then I'm off the charts!"

"That's not true."

"Give me that thing," Stuart said, grabbing the receiver from me. "I don't know who the hell you are, but I plan to find out. Now, I am the husband. Joan is my wife. Is that clear? *Is* it?"

I tried to take the receiver from him. "Get your hands off," he said.

I ran upstairs to the other phone. "Gil?"

"Is he on retainer, or do you hire him by the hour? I thought you were going to tell him you belong to me. Go ahead, *tell* him!"

"You madman!" Stuart roared, "I told you she was *my wife! Mine!*"

"Please!" I wailed. "Let me—"

"Shut up!" Stuart interrupted.

Gil pursued. "Well, *tell* him who you belong to!"

"I—" I stopped myself short. What was going on? *Belong* to? Was I chattel? "I belong to *me*! What are you doing? Fighting over the keys to a goddamn car or something?"

"I *knew* you wouldn't answer the question, you whoring bitch!" Gil raved.

I heard a door open. John had come from his bedroom. "The TV woke me up, mommy."

"I'm sorry, honey. It's off now," I sang, hoping he was too sleepy to catch the delirious lilt. He went back to his bedroom.

Returning to the kitchen, I saw that Stuart had hung up.

"What the hell was that all about?" He glowered at me. "Talk!"

"I can't now."

"What?"

"I won't."

"Joan!" Imperative.

"In the morning. I feel crazy now. The whole thing is a mix-up."

"I can't believe this!" He looked as though he might strike me.

"Stuart," I said, intending to warn him.

"I can't think clearly now," he said, backing off, leaving the room.

I poured a glass of orange juice, which I couldn't drink, then sat at the kitchen table.

From down the basement, the whirring sound of the exercise bike droned on and on as Stuart pedalled his way to nowhere.

Noon, Sunday, the children were out riding their bikes and I was putting together a brunch for Stuart and myself while he cross-examined me. The fateful call seemed like a bad dream, though its effects on me were real enough. With the two men as my contenders, I had seen myself as independent of them both. I was in my own corner, my own promoter. For the moment, at least, I felt tough.

Standing at the screen door, between questions, I was watching the changing patterns of light in the branches of our maple. It was a Renoir day, all sunlight and color. My loss, not to be out there, trying to capture something of it on canvas. What would I do? A wash of greens and yellows, creating an impression of impermanence? Maybe work on a crisper image, or abstract.

The day was too beautiful for me to cast a shadow over it, and my life, with lies.

I confessed my affair with Gil in response to Stuart's next question: "You say it was a lucky *guess,* his knowing about that freckle?"

I went on scrambling eggs as Stuart assimilated the facts, his level-headed self again. I wondered if, in the end, he would consider me an asset rather than a liability. And what if he did. I would not resign myself to a lifetime of "making do" anymore.

He looked pensive. Was he wondering how to tell me that he had run out of clean socks and would I wash them before he packed his bags? "We never laughed enough," I suddenly thought aloud. "I was either being squelched or laughing by myself."

"I'll stay in that back room at the office for the time being," said

Stuart. "I'll contact you regarding financial and other matters. There's no need to make this affair any more mindless than you've already managed to do."

A bird swooped by the window. "We're not enemies," I mused, removing the pan from the burner. "But we're just not—well, I mean you should have known about that freckle yourself."

"I'm out of clean socks. I would appreciate your putting through a wash before I go."

"Certainly."

"You have no discipline."

"On the contrary. I kept myself in check ever since I can remember. We haven't laughed together—don't you understand? We've had *circumstances* in common. Not *energies*. I was a frustrated bitch. Do you want toast?"

"Please."

"About time I opened the box and let myself out."

The phone rang. It was Zenia. Just what I needed. "I got your number from Dusty." Her voice was so very musical. "I hope I'm not disturbing you?"

"No, no. How are you?" I asked, trying not to reflect tension in my voice.

"Well, you see, Sonny—you know, Son Kim, my photographer? —Sonny was developing some of the films today?"

I dropped the bread into the toaster. "Yes?"

"And he says that he'd like to shoot our scene over so he can use it in his new book. You know, the one where we—"

"Yes, yes." I spooned the eggs into the plates. "What about it?"

"He didn't get the exact atmosphere he wanted. There was too much background interference and too much moving around. You know what I mean?"

Stuart frowned. "Who is this on the phone *now*, if you don't mind my asking?"

I turned to him. "It's my friend, Zenia." I spoke into the receiver. "Sorry—what were you saying? He wants to shoot the scene over? But I'm afraid I'm not quite ready for publication. I was a little high last night and, well—"

"Who *is* this Zenia?" asked Stuart.

Zenia sighed. "But it's really a shame, Joan. Your breasts are really photogenic. They have character. *Really.* Sonny says so, too."

"Well?" said Stuart.

"Excuse me." I turned to him again. "She's a model. We posed together last night. She says my breasts have character."

Stuart choked on his egg. "Forget the toast," he coughed.

"I'm flattered, Zenia, but maybe you had better find someone else. Thanks for thinking of me, anyway. Maybe another time. Right. Bye."

Stuart rose from the table as the sound of the children's sunny laughter drifted to us through the screen door.

Later that day, I thought, or possibly tomorrow, I would see about picking up my art supplies at Gil's.

After a hasty and inadequate explanation to the children (mommy and daddy have to iron out their little differences, etc.), Stuart left to set up temporary residence in his office suite. He went off appropriately depressed and remote, with a list of tidying-up chores he had to accomplish sticking out of the jacket pocket of his suit. I felt sorry for him, and a rending feeling of regret that accompanies the loss of anything possessed for a long time, regardless of the quality of ownership. I thought that his first nights would be the most difficult, the loneliest, the strangest—and that I would experience the kind of anxiety that goes with Confirmations, Bar Mitzvahs, Sweet Sixteens, Graduations and other occasions that mark passages from which there is no turning back.

Stuart was already out of the house when Gil came wheeling up the driveway with my big canvases sticking out of his trunk. I watched him from upstairs, behind the curtain in Laura's room, as he untied the rope and began removing the contents of the trunk. The easel and paints were in the back seat and he piled them next to the canvases. I wanted an excuse to run downstairs with a "Hey, watch how you handle my stuff" or a "Get your goddamn paws off the wet paint!"—*some* excuse that would project me downstairs and out of the house and within reach. But he was especially careful in the way he handled everything, even going so far as to bring it all around to the back deck. I ran from one window to another, watching him divest himself of my things. I was like an outlaw, darting from one hiding place to another. But I just couldn't *appear*.

When the last of my belongings was on the deck, he looked up at the house. My heart beat fast. *Start* something, damn it! I want to scream back! Make me take after you! He started to walk to the door, then hesitated, then began walking away. I ran to Laura's open window and saw him approach his car. A barbaric cry was stuck in my throat. I watched him hesitate again. Just before he got into the car he shook his fist at the house. "BITCH!"

I didn't start crying until late afternoon, and then I couldn't stop.

12

"Joan? Joan Wolf!"

I looked up. I'd been sitting on a bench outside the Parrish Museum in Southampton, among the busts of the Caesars, thinking about my new independent status and feeling unmoored, rather than launched. "Carolyn Taylor! Jesus!" I jumped up and hugged her. Had it been thirteen years?

Carolyn examined me at arm's length. "You look marvelous! And it's Stevens."

"So do you! And mine's Hiller."

"I simply can't believe it. What are you doing here? I saw you from the street. I thought for a moment it was Hamlet."

I could see her point. "Was I lost in space? I—uh—I've just been to the exhibit."

"I saw it yesterday. What a bore! Another one of their panoramas of Nineteenth Century Americana."

I drew her down. "Come and talk. Tell me about yourself."

We sat on the bench spouting autobiographical précis and I remembered how we used to sit together cross-legged under the gnarled tree outside our dorm, reviewing English 300 and our love life, such as it was.

133

Carolyn was wearing a flouncy skirt and loosely-laced bodice. Her skin was smooth and poreless; her hair, long and fine, pinned up in a fashionable sweep. She was a cultivated flower.

We tried to catch up with time, regretting, predictably, that we hadn't kept in touch. She was from a different orbit of class and wealth, to which she returned during intercessions and permanently upon graduation. I was out of her league, hampered by the ordinary obstacles of life, like having to price a new oil burner or foregoing a trip to the orient. She was constrained by fancy and mortality. She had been a bright student, especially in the languages and literature and had acquired more than the finishing school sheen typified by the other orchids of our class.

I learned that she had met her present and third husband, while he was between wives, on a cruise. He was a leather importer on a grand scale, forever on the move, and she was dabbling in her father's business, as a consultant to an international cosmetics firm. "I anticipated plums and grapes when tangerine was the going blush and he put me to work at once."

"My—husband is a C.P.A. I work part time in a real estate agency. Stifle the yawn. I've been painting again."

She didn't yawn. In fact she *insisted* that she was tired of being a chic hostess in a childless duplex to a husband who simply needed a home base and a pause between mistresses. "I hardly ever see the man. He may be an agent for the C.I.A. for all I know. I used to enjoy gallivanting around the world. Now all that's left of the wanderlust is the lust. I just bought a place here in Southampton. I'm thinking of becoming a hausfrau."

I doubted it. "Actually, my husband just moved out. I've 'let him down,' as he'd put it."

" 'What to ourselves in passion we propose, the passion ending, doth the purpose lose.' Have you been remiss in the apple pie department?"

"It . . . wasn't in passion proposed in the first place."

"Aha. You've been indiscreet and your husband is a pious man."

I felt guilty. After all, Stuart was a good boy, a responsible

134

fellow. It was a remake of the think-of-the-starving-children-in-India bit. So the brisket was dry and tasteless. Eat it and be grateful. "Well, yes."

"Are you in love?"

"I don't know if I trust my judgment." What did it matter? I'd probably never see him again, anyway.

"Trust the heart. If it all signifies nothing, then at least enjoy the sound and fury."

I thought of the afternoons we had spent as versifying under-graduates. "'Gather ye rosebuds while ye may. Old time is still a-flying'?"

Carolyn leaned towards me and whispered, "'And this same flower that smiles today, tomorrow will be dying.' It appears that I would like a dose of hearth and home, and you of flying the coop. Incidentally, your hair is fabulous. I recall the tail."

"I remember you with the long braid and the fantastic Mexican belt."

"Do you? I still have it somewhere."

"I thought you had everything," I said. "That you had it made in every conceivable way."

"Sure. Do you remember that poem by Parker—'Comment'?"

"The only Parker I remember is the pen."

"'Oh, life is a glorious cycle of song, a medley of extemporanea; and love is a thing that can never go wrong; and I am Marie of Roumania.' So much for your assessment. Have you eaten lunch? Why don't you come by for a visit? I have a facial in fifteen minutes at Arden's. We can meet—let me see—at twelve thirty at my place."

"I'd love to. I was going to buy the kids some school clothes and then—sure."

Carolyn gave me directions. "It looks like a spaceship. You can't miss it."

No, I couldn't have. Ten minutes early, I pulled into its circular drive. It was a cool, modern design in natural ash—open to the heavens through a large plastic dome. It sat atop a hill overlooking the ocean. Adequate digs for Carolyn to enjoy her taste of "hearth and home." I parked between a white Rolls Royce and a van marked Job's Cleaners We're The Best and walked around the spaceship to the deck facing the ocean. Stretching out before it were the dunes—stark and lovely argument for building regulations. The oceanfront footage was nothing like this in Hampton Village, where the precious beach was being wasted by overbuilding and underprotecting. What did the hot-shot grabbers care about land exploitation, the County bigwigs about capturing littoral drift?

In the yard off the deck a large metal free form bent gracefully toward the ocean. Atop its highest curve, a bird had perched to admire the view. It flew off as I walked across the deck to the sliding glass doors. I could see the expanse of dining and living room, all earth and sand tones, from the door. Draped over an armchair was a plastic-wrapped delivery from what I assumed to be Job's Cleaners We're The Best. I supposed Carolyn had heard my footsteps, because she cried "Come!" just as I was about to knock on the glass.

I slid open the door and as I crossed the threshold I realized that the exclamation had not been intended for me, for it was followed by a throaty cry together with a low grunt coming from a couch about ten feet away on whose back I fixed my gaze. A slender foot appeared briefly over the top of the couch. Then a young man (The Best?) rose from its depths, zipping his fly. He looked like someone out of Fleetwood Mac, and he gasped when he saw me.

Carolyn stood up, unlaced but unflappable. Her cheeks were a delicate pink from her facial and/or whatever had just been happening. As the young man slipped past me Carolyn cocked her head to one side and smiled wryly. "'I have numbered the minutes so heavy and slow, till of that dissipation I tire, and as for exciting amusements,—you know, one can't *always* be stirring the fire.'"

Christ . What a memory.

Up until this point in my life I had lain with only three men. Judging from the look of nonchalance on Carolyn's face when I walked in on her and the delivery boy, she had stopped counting long ago.

Although I never approached her casualness, in the weeks ahead I did become more relaxed regarding statistics.

My move toward sexual freedom was a decision more than an inclination. I defied my longing for Gil—still painfully strong—by defiling it. My dance of independence was meant to stifle this mono-directed yearning as well as disclaim it as a moral imperative. If a man attracted me and the situation were convenient, I challenged myself to turn whim into deed. Why? I asked myself. Why *not?* came the audacious reply.

In the meantime, I painted. The spark had been ignited and the flame burned on its own now. Painting, my monogamy, gave me joy and structured my days.

I had a number of interesting encounters during those weeks of "summer magic," perhaps none more appropriate to my plunge into the sea of independence than my maiden voyage around Shelter Island on a Tartan 27.

It all began at the annual two-day Hampton Village sidewalk art show in which I finally decided to enter. It was a public statement of self-acknowledgment. I brought along some large oils and a stack of pastel drawings. I'd spent long hours, especially on the canvases, and yet I didn't think they looked overworked. I relied on suggestions rather than detail—had to get angles and balances just right. In the painting of a woman on a swing it was only after I had separated and broken the strokes of three of her toes that the exuberance of being thrown into space was suddenly apparent and I was satisfied. My favorite painting was still the one I'd planned on the beach, that afternoon with Sue. The dancing figures. It was one of the paintings I'd worked on at Gil's. It was not for sale. The pastels were a kind of chimerical vision of childhood inspired by real memories. After I sold one, I realized how much I enjoyed the approval of others and tried to reproach myself for it.

My stall was on Main Street, across from Steele's Pharmacy.

137

To my right a bearded, hearty-looking watercolorist sat on his folding bridge chair, graciously accepting frequent praise and rare payment for his series of Montauk scenes. To my left a diligent, middle-aged man was stationed, burning personalized logos into wooden plaques.

For two unusually hot days I watched the colorful array of art observers and their appendages admiring and muttering, crowding and bumping, bargaining and pondering their way from exhibit to exhibit—all supporting, regardless of individual aesthetic preferences, the smart young capitalists who carted around freezers of ice pops and soft drinks in their little red wagons. It was the summer's largest gathering of year-rounders and transients. I saw Beth and Pat, players from my winter tennis group, who invited me to play doubles with them on Pat's new clay court. They cooed over my paintings, but said they had already spent their "allowances" on "what's-his-name's stranded row boats." Our conversation was brief, for their children were tugging at them and their husbands were striding out of sight. Mr. McGuinness and Mr. Devon cruised by, hand in hand in spirit only, and admired one of my oils for its strong colors and sense of balance. Dusty Bantom, delighted to see that I was "so terribly imaginative and free," purchased a framed pastel of children playing ball and kissed me on my cheek.

After I returned from one of my breaks on the second day (my wood-logo-burner-neighbor guarded the "merchandise" while I grabbed a bite to eat) I found an earnest looking man—fifty-ish, gray-bearded, attractive though a bit on the portly side—examining my pastels, head tilted, drawing on his pipe, tapping his foot. "May I help you?" I inquired.

He was startled. "Er—yes." He looked me up and down, clearly preferring the down. "Are you the artist?"

"Well, I'm the painter."

"I'm not sure modesty becomes you. Do you suppose you would have the time or inclination to illustrate someone *else's* ideas on demand?"

"Perhaps. Why?"

"Sorry." He drew his hand from out of the pocket of his dungaree jacket and extended it towards me. "I'm Jeffrey Kane. I write. Recently, children's books." He flashed a charming, tobacco stained smile at me. "I like your work, Joan, especially the pastels. They go well with my style—seated in reality but a bit unearthly." He pulled at his beard. "Perhaps you could exaggerate the phantasmagoric quality in a series of drawings for me?"

"Is this a proposition?"

He raised his peppered brow and sucked in on his pipe. "A proposal, rather. Perhaps we'll get to propositions another time." Smooth, very smooth.

I remembered seeing his name. It was on the cover of one of John's books. "You did some out-of-the-world account of a boy's dream."

"Yes. *Timothy's Trials.* I didn't care for the art work, though. Too self-conscious and static. This stuff has movement. It's simple and poetic without being ethereal. It's got substance. It's not ... lacy. Although it's a different medium, the line reminds me of Matisse. This is more mystical, of course."

"Don't embarrass me. My pretensions aren't so grand."

"Unless the Whitney made you an offer you couldn't resist," he laughed.

"We—ell—" I was beginning to feel the nodule of a career.

"Actually, you know, a friend of mine owns a gallery in Bridgehampton—"

"The Nelson?"

"Yes. Sally Nelson. She'd really go for your oils. She loves the big, fauvistic style. Perhaps she'd consider your canvases for her next show. Would you be agreeable?"

"Of course!" The nodule was swelling.

"Well, then. Now that we've established a partnership, how about going for a sail with me and my hosts? I've been procrastinating, coward that I am, and I think they're beginning to suspect. They've gotten me to go along with them only once."

It seems that Jeffrey Kane was visiting the summer home of friends, the vice president of a New York ad agency and his wife.

Although their house was on the bay side of Dune Road, they preferred sailing the deeper waters off the north fork and had therefore docked their Tartan in New Suffolk. Their guest had chosen to remain dry docked that day, and had missed a trip around Nassau Point, but had promised to accompany them on their next excursion in a day or two. "How about it?" he asked. "I'm sure the Hubbards would love to have you. We can talk business another time."

It sounded like fun. Fun was just what I required my social life to provide me with. I was seeking to replace Gil not with a comparable relationship, but with a variety of diversions, which would attest to my freedom.

Jeffrey and I exchanged telephone numbers, and shook hands fondly. As he strolled off and I waved to his receding figure, I saw Gil, of all people, staring at me from a vantage point three exhibits away. How long had he been posted there? From his posture I was sure he had seen my latest transaction. Something caught me, like a blow, in the pit of my stomach and I was tempted to run to him and throw myself at his feet. But did I want to face the inevitable scene of petty vindictiveness when I was feeling so high?

Gil helped make my decision by turning away and walking off in a dejected slump.

Son of a bitch.

13

I had never gone sailing before. Who knew about storm jibs and reefing, luffing and jibbing, heeling and tacking? I thought I was going on a romantic cruise with Jeffrey Kane and his slick urban friends. Who knew that the smiling ad man would turn into a mad tyrant on board his vessel with the excuse of "running a tight ship"?

They picked me up at 6:15 in the morning, an hour my bleary-eyed sitter found ungodly. In the car we were all right. From my house the trip to New Suffolk took about forty-five minutes and although later I would be kicking myself for not having reviewed my will, we spent a pleasant drive chatting about the differences between city and country living, commercial and fine arts, and open and closed enrollment. Dick and Vera Hubbard seemed like an all-American couple, having arrived at success through their own devices while still retaining their collegiate idealism. In their late thirties and still in the flush of youth, these flaxen look-alikes seemed the picture of health and harmony. Numbskull that I was, I assumed that their seafaring roles would be consistent with their dry dock personas. The trunk was glutted with "foul weather gear" (not for today, please!), and Jeffrey and I shared the rear of their "junk-hauling" Chevy with the sandwiches and fruit, a tool box, a sail that had been repaired, a tide table, and various charts of Long Island Sound and the Peconic Bays. Jeffrey alluded to his plans for our project only briefly, postponing a serious talk for another day. "I have to admit," he whispered, lighting his pipe and eyeing my denim thigh among the charts, "I don't enjoy mixing business and pleasure." (He tried moving his jean-clad leg closer to mine, but a yellow freezer stood in his way.)

We arrived at the dock at 7:00 A.M. and we were immediately put to work unloading the car and loading the boat. My morning coffee was beginning to cause stress to my bladder and I was becoming concerned about where I would be allowed to pee, since there was no ladies room in sight. I asked where the nearest facility was located and got the first hint that Dick was going to consider me a non sea-worthy pain in the ass. "I'm afraid you'll have to wait until we're under sail," he said, feigning concern. "The dock owner is not here this weekend, otherwise you might have been able to use his john." I bit my lip and handed him his tool box. He was standing in the rear tub ("it's the cockpit, Joan!") of the boat, and reached up towards the dock where I was standing. Alas! He happened to notice my clogs, obviously a crime worse than mutiny and punishable by death! "You have Topsiders, I hope!"

"Um—no, I—"

"You've brought sneakers, at least, for god's sake!"

"Well, no."

"You'll have to go barefoot. Unsafe and slippery but better than *those* things."

I tried to be friendly. "This is really a beautiful, sleek boat. How long is it?"

"Twenty-seven feet."

"Hence 'Tartan 27.' Sorry I'm so ignorant."

"Just take off your shoes right now please." I obeyed.

As we were piling into the cockpit I could see that we were going to be in very close quarters indeed, unless one or two of us chose to go inside, down the steps ("below!"), the thought of which made me queasy. Unlike the motor boat ("stink pot!") of about equal length docked next to the Hubbard's, the sailboat had little room on deck to accommodate people, most of it being taken up with masts and other fittings. We were to sit in the cockpit area in the rear ("stern!") of the boat and shift our weight from left to right ("port to starboard!") as we wove ("tacked!") our way around the southern tip of Robin's Island (which, judging from the chart, looked like a leaf surrounded by a huge body of water), then proceed east to and around Shelter Island, then back to New Suffolk where we might, if we were still on speaking terms, have a bite of supper at the Fisherman's Haven.

The *Verdict* (a combination of "Vera" and "Dick" I assumed but was afraid to ask) was ready to push out. But first we had to put on extremely uncomfortable, cumbersome life jackets provided by the captain. Once imprisoned inside my kapok chest, I said goodbye to whatever romantic notions I was foolish enough to still have. They were rapidly replaced by the notions (Kierkegaard pops to mind) of fear and trembling. Jeffrey, not exactly a first mate type, but more experienced than I, was requested to put out and stow his pipe, then fetch a horn to blow as we made our way out of the harbor into the bay, in order to warn blind boats entering. Between all these precautions and the pressure of my morning cups, I was ready to pee in my pants.

Dick started the engine (a modest inboard, to be used only before hoisting the sails in the open bay, or, I supposed, in the event of an extended calm). Using the steering stick ("tiller!") he backed us out of the parking space ("slip!") as his wife drew the lines that had secured us to the dock.

We were on our way.

For a while, once the sails were hoisted and the accompanying orders were barked, I enjoyed myself. When the noisy engine was shut off and we were suddenly and quietly moving with the wind, carried along by the elements—thrust defeating constraint—the feeling was delicious. Space, freedom, smooth drive, warm breeze, seagulls, and silence overcame the binding forces of life jackets and personalities and made me feel bare and at one with

143

the universe. However, this was not to last. In the narrow space between the south shore of Robins Island and the north shore of Southampton there is a fast, strong current, akin to a bottleneck, called the South Race. This is where we started tipping over ("heeling!") like mad and I remembered my bladder and the unwritten clauses that should have been in my last will and testament. "Do we ever lose sight of land?" I queried sweetly, after a particularly nasty angle change ("jibe!") in which the horizontal pole ("boom!") came close to decapitating me. Dick looked disgusted. Whatever qualities in a woman he preferred on land, coyness was certainly not one of his on-deck favorites. "I hope not," he answered tartly, as Vera sent me a furtive look of warning.

Dick decided to shorten ("reef!") the "main sheet" and exchange the "Genoa," suitable for light air, for the "heavy weather jib." Jeffrey, looking frightfully calm or quietly frightened, tried to stabilize himself by holding onto the railing ("pulpit!") Vera, perched on the edge of her ass and muttering obscenities, worked the tiller while Dick did a balancing act at the bow, undoing shackles and cleats, or whatever, and hollering commands. "Into the wind, Vera! . . . Let the main sheet luff while I get this damn jib unfolded! . . . Into the wind! Into the wind! . . . Fall off! Fall off! . . . Terrible! . . . Wonderful! . . . You're screwing us up! . . . Good job!"

"May I please go Below and use the Head?" I asked Vera, whose eyes were glued to the horizon as she manipulated the tiller, trying to follow what seemed to me to be a battery of conflicting orders. "I think it's really absolutely necessary." Hmmm. Maybe I'll take a quick vomit, too.

"Go ahead, go ahead, but read the directions on the door carefully," snapped Vera. What? I had to be told how to *urinate,* yet?

Dick was teetering his way back to the cockpit as I was faltering down the three steep steps. Once below, I became even more frightened of this wild heeling we were experiencing. It seemed to me that we were on the verge of capsizing, although Dick and Vera had both assured me that we could be in danger of no such thing with the stable Tartan. We seemed to be listing at a ninety degree angle with the active seas but I had been reassured that we could do no such thing. (The illusion, however, was quite real.) I stumbled through the kitchen ("galley!") to the head and opened the door. Oh no! I could see only *water* out of the porthole—the angle was preposterous. Out of the porthole at the opposite side, in the galley, I could see only sky! In spite of my terror, I read the directions for flushing on the inside of the door of the head, and realized at once that my I.Q. was inadequate for this task. In my nervous state I had no idea when to pull *UP* the pump lever, when to *PUMP* the pump lever, when to make sure the pump lever is *DOWN,* how to fill up or empty the fucking toilet into which I was supposed to aim my ass in all this turmoil.

"Make sure you read the directions!" Dick called to me, reinforcing his wife's advice. "You could flood the boat if you keep the pump . . ."

I couldn't hear the next words. I had to go fast. Directions later. I shut the door as Dick was loudly explaining how "to keep us in a close hauled tack!" and, in the small closet, tried to balance myself and lower my pants at the same time. No small task while hampered by an awkward life jacket! I hadn't locked the door and it kept swinging open and banging shut with the movement of the boat, but I didn't care. I just wanted to get this over with. Once my pants were down I crouched, with as much accuracy as I could, over the toilet, holding onto the grip on the wall undoubtedly there for just that purpose. With a mixture of fear and relief, I gushed my insides out while on the brink of either falling into the toilet or out the door. My pants still folded over my feet, I again tried to interpret the list of directions on the door. I pulled the pump lever up. But the repercussions, if I should be in error, were too immense. "Help!" I called, finally, trying both to pull up my pants and to prevent the sea and pee from overflowing the bowl. "Help!"

"I'm coming!" called Jeffrey, who was hopefully better at understanding directions under stress than I. I tried to hike up my pants, but was unable to quickly enough. Jeffrey appeared, wide-eyed but in command (rather like a fifteen year old gynecol-ogist) and pumped out the bowl while we bumped together in the small space. "See?" he said. "One must be sure to leave the lever down—like *so*—or else the water will continue to enter through the open valve."

"Thank you," I mumbled, covering myself with my free hand (the other was clutching the grip).

Suddenly, Jeffrey started to undo his pants. Gee, did he have to go, too? Yes, it seemed, but only as a preparatory gesture. Once having pumped out his own liquid waste, he excused himself and grabbed my behind.

"Everything under control?" called Dick from the cockpit.

"Yes, indeed!" called Jeffrey, thrusting a hand between my legs. "I hope you don't mind," he panted. "You're really irresisti-ble with that big orange vest and nothing on below it."

I lost my balance and fell onto the toilet as he continued to fondle me, his own jacket becoming an encumbrance in these efforts. The boat pitched and I was thrown forward, towards him. We went tumbling out the door, I falling on top of him. Squeezing between my thighs, then pushing them apart, he tried to invade the harbor, as our life jackets prevented the body contact most often associated with this sort of intimacy. We scrambled on the floor in the small area between the head and the pantry closet, inching our way to the cramped front space ("hold!") of the boat. My life-fearing anxiety and Jeffrey's ener-getic maneuvers were combining to form an unusual, but titillat-ing experience. I ended up sitting on top of him, my pants lying in a heap around one of my feet. We were half in and half out of the hold and his mast was half in and half out of my cockpit (circum-stances made insertion a challenge), when Vera surprised me with her presence. My back was facing the steps leading below, and I did not hear the stealthy tread of her Topsiders as she approached us. "Some bunch of mates *you* are!" she exclaimed, with some of the relaxed charm she had shown in the old Chevy.

Then, without a moment's hesitation, the sport climbed over our lurching bodies, removed her pants, spread her knees and dropped anchor over Jeffrey's open and eager face. Meanwhile, the *Verdict* was rolling along and I was having a devil of a time keeping his rudder from flying out from under me. Sitting upright and holding fast seemed to be the most practical method.

Is this really happening to me, I thought. Are we in some kind of dadaist movie? Is this what they call the "easy life"?

Vera and I were shimmying over Jeffrey fore and aft, gaining momentum. Vera's back was to me. I was watching Jeffrey's peppery beard twitch. I was concentrating, in this manner, on attaining a climax when I was distracted by a flurry of movement at my rear hatch. I could feel hands stroking me, then see them when they swept around to caress my belly. The sensations were not unpleasant. I focused my body's attention on this agreeable activity.

Hold it! Double take! Quick recount of personnel!

"Who's steering the boat?" I cried, swiveling around.

Dick rose to a standing position on the step. He was no longer wearing his white shorts. "I've got us on the *autopilot!*" he explained, swaying over us. "Can't you hear it? There isn't a boat approaching our course and we are perfectly safe." He stepped down and hovered over us.

"Come here, Dick," Vera said. He moved toward her. She reached around and calmly grabbed his tiller, gently navigated him toward her gyrating form, and secured him between her jaws. "Not to worry," he said, clutching at his wife's head and thrusting his hips at her. "We are sailing on a straight course . . . AAAH! . . . no tacking necessary . . . MMM! . . . perfectly safe."

The boat listed in a sudden swell. Jeffrey let out a muffled grunt. This sent a tremor through Vera's body, which caused a jolt to Dick's pelvis. This, in turn, caused Dick to lose his footing, and he fell over backwards.

Within a very short time we were in a state of total confusion among the sail bags and sundries in the hold. I was blindly feeling around, trying to latch onto any free appendange that would transport me to what had been my imminent orgasm. I caught an unidentified flying organ and guided it into port. It discharged as I

147

fluttered in my own release. Peering out from under what I imagined to be either a tarpaulin or an empty sail bag, I discovered that it was Dick whom I had to thank for my unusual climax. Jeffrey, meanwhile, was busily coming inside the aperture Dick had vacated in the melee, while Vera was fingering her own abandoned vessel.

So much for romance on the high seas.

We were shortly shipshape, dressed and on deck, consuming our salami and roast beef sandwiches (except for Jeffrey, whose roughriding orgasm had backfired on him and who was now at half-mast and barfing overboard—Dick: "Into the wind, damn it, or it will blow back in your face!").

Once again, Dick was at the helm. He disengaged the autopilot and reasserted his dictatorial role by reprimanding Vera for dropping potato chip crumbs onto his precious deck and perhaps into his precious bilge. She, in turn, mumbled a salty curse, but in the submissive tone befitting her station.

We had another buoyant, pleasant run, the sails filled with mild, warm air, the smell of summer sea life all around us, our gentle wake soothing my fear of death and jellyfish and Jeffrey's upset stomach. That is, until, off the north shore of Shelter Island, we almost collided with a ferryboat on its shuttle trip to Greenport. I was, at the time, holding the tiller while Dick, in the manner befitting a commander, was telling me how to keep the sails luffing as he unreefed the mainsail. Vera, standing at the bow, her flaxen hair blowing free like the ribbons ("telltales!") high on the mast, suddenly issued an unruffled warning that I was to avoid the oncoming ferry. This simple utterance seemed to paralyze my ability to reason, and as Dick bellowed commands, I froze.

He jumped down into the cockpit and grabbed the tiller from me. "You'll have us in irons!" he roared. "Leeward! Leeward!"

Mutiny. I hurried (downstairs!) through the (kitchen!) to the (small front room!) where I huddled with my anger and fear.

After the disaster was averted, the ferry circumnavigated, Dick begged forgiveness for being impatient (actually, Jeffrey apologized *for* him and, as I discovered, without his knowledge) and I returned to the deck and remained there, hurt and dishevelled, for the rest of the trip back.

The ship's clock rang twice as we were pulling into the slip in New Suffolk. I cheated and looked down at my watch. It was five o'clock. After a half hour of compulsive boat tidying, rope arranging, securing and double-checking the above, our party was ready to make amends at the Fisherman's Haven.

Dick, released from the spell of the captain's domain, was able to put on the cloak of good humor so familiar to friend and colleague. Hence Vera was able to recover her healthy calm. Our meal turned out to be a social truce; a palatable failure. My feelings were fatigued and neutral; my scallops, tough.

The Hubbards dropped me at the foot of my driveway and waited in the car as Jeffrey walked me to the door.

"Will I see you tomorrow?" he asked, smoothing his beard. "I can bring over my text and you can begin work as soon as we decide on advance and royalties." He was certainly more at ease on land, with the fire hazard, his pipe, once again gripped comfortably between his teeth.

"You know—what you said about not mixing business with pleasure?" I said, brushing my salty, sticky hair out of my stinging eyes.

"Yes?" he smiled, taking my hand most graciously in his two.

"Forget the pleasure. Let's stick to business."

The sex I had experienced aboard our ship of fools had been about as inappropriate to the subject of self realization as I had encountered. Inanity, I would later learn, was not the worst form of irrelevance.

149

14

Jeffrey agreed accommodatingly to stick to business, and my career was launched in the noonday sun on the redwood deck the very next day, amidst the chatter of my children and the buzz of my neighbor's lawn mower. Actually, I think Jeffrey was *relieved* to have been let off the sexual hook. While we were having a glass of iced tea and arranging our next meeting he whipped out his wallet and displayed about six or seven photographs of his wife, his children, and his little grandchild, the tears welling up in his eyes as he told me of their histories and feats, stressing that none of the photos did any of them justice. He said he had been briefly separated from his wife, but, I gathered from his exhibition, that he had had his little recess and was going home, tail between his legs.

During the days that followed, I worked like a demon. My marriage, like my tennis game, was suspended in a state of amicable quiescence. Stuart occasionally called to inquire after a bank balance or the children's health (thank goodness he had not yet questioned my maternal or material capabilities). He was now ensconced in an airy little apartment in Hampton Bays and was, I imagined, writing lists and avoiding issues. He sent us subsistence money and beach presents for Laura and John, whom he occasionally took out to lunch, but who knew when a lawyer would get him by the balls and turn our structured nonrelationship into chaotic ill will?

The weekend after I began illustrating Jeffrey's unusual story, entitled *Voyage to Outer Dilutia,* Susan telephoned. I hadn't spoken to her for weeks.

Susan had found out about my separated state through my mother's helper, of all people. "I was shocked," she said, in a tone somehow unconvincing. "How did it happen? Why haven't you spoken to me?" She sounded quivery, off balance.

"I've been preoccupied. Sorry I've been so out of touch lately. And how have *you* been?"

"Fair. Very fair. Actually—I know it seems selfish of me—but I was thinking of taking you up on that offer you made—when was it, June?—of taking the kids for a day or two?"

"I'd love to," I cooed unwillingly. "No trouble. You and Roger need a break."

There was a pause. Then, "Never mind. Never mind. It was a stupid idea."

"Don't be silly. When will you bring Bobby and Bill over?"

"Tonight? But *really*—"

"Terrific. Laura and John will be thrilled."

"Thanks, Joan."

"This will be good for both of you." I was already thinking of ways to amuse Bobby the Whirlwind to keep him from destroying the place. Perhaps I could tie him to the bedpost with a two-day supply of pretzels and coloring books. . . .

"See you later," I chirped.

It suddenly dawned on me that she hadn't pursued the subject of my separation.

Sunday night found me exhausted. After bouncing the heart out of the box springs, the children had finally fallen asleep. I was sitting barefoot in the kitchen in an old robe, leafing through a magazine. Where was Susan, anyway? She had said she would be back late afternoon. It was already 11:30!

There was a knock at the front door and I assumed it must be she. I hurried to the door. I opened it with a smile. The smile froze on my face and I instinctively clutched the robe to my body.

"Uh, hello Roger."

Roger kicked the door shut and planted himself before me, his hands on his hips, looking like the Green Giant straddling a bad crop.

"You've come to pick up the children?" I asked, backing up into my Early American den, still hugging myself protectively.

Roger followed me into the den, glaring out at me from beneath his furrowed brow, his thin lips curling downward. "Well, you've finally done it," he snarled, taking an ominous step towards me.

"What? *What* did I do?

"You put your fucking ideas into my wife's head, that's what you did!"

"What are you talking about?"

"Do you know where Susan was this weekend?" He removed his hands from his hips. His arms hung at his side, like weapons. "She was with your husband!"

It surprised me that the idea was painless, that my spiritual divorce from Stuart was so conclusive. "And you're blaming me? What kind of ideas did I put into her head to make this happen?"

"I know she's talked about getting jobs and independence—all that emancipation crap—with you."

"You have a way with words," I said. "Why don't you sit down. Do you want a cup of tea or something?" It seemed like an inappropriate question, but the event had no precedent.

He sat down. I followed his example. "How do you *know* about Stuart and Susan?" I asked.

"Because she just came home and told me, *that's* how."

No questions about reliable evidence here. "Did you want that cup of tea?"

"No."

There was a pause, during which I realized that I must be looking something of a wreck and both the fact and my concern with it annoyed me.

"One minute she's afraid I'll walk out on her," he said. "Next minute she's got to get out and start a life for herself because she's too dependent on me. Then she's crying that I don't think she's an exciting woman, that maybe getting a job or going to school will make her exciting to me. Does this ring a bell?"

"It sounds like she's unhappy and confused."

"That's your department," he said. "Then, when I tell her it's not true, that I love her the way she is, she says maybe she should get a job anyway, for her own self-respect, or some damn crap."

I looked down at the open magazine, at an ad for girdles, and instinctively closed it. "How did you tell her you love her the way she is? By telling her if she gets a job she's abandoning you and the kids? I'm sure you showed a lot of compassion."

"How the hell would *you* know how I behaved?"

"I'm guessing."

"You put ideas into her head. Then you set a great example for her, and all womankind, by screwing around with some teacher or other—I heard about *that* from Stuart! To top it off you tell all, leaving your husband no alternative but to get the hell out of the house. Where does that leave him? It leaves him feeling real good, doesn't it? In fact, what it does is prime him for another woman! And who do you think that is? That's right. Susan. You made it all come true, baby. I've just come to thank you." He placed his hand over mine.

I started to slip my hand away but he held on to it. "Roger. For god's sake. Don't you think your being unfaithful to her had anything to do with her unhappiness, her . . . infidelity?"

He wouldn't let go of my hand. "My *what?* She told you about—"

"She was very unhappy."

"How can you compare—"

154

"Your . . . fooling around . . . and her adultery don't have the same point value in your game, do they? She broke the rules of the game, didn't she?"

"Goddamn it!" He was thoroughly distraught.

"Look, Roger," I said, "can I say something to you? Sue and I are different. I'm sure her act of infidelity was an act of confusion. Because she loves you so much it was probably her first dishonest lay. My affair with . . . the teacher . . . was an act of enlightenment. He was my first *honest* lay."

Roger stared at me in disbelief. "Is this the way you talk to Sue?"

"Are you a prude, Roger?"

"Well, we know you're not, don't we?"

He rose from the table, never letting go of my hand.

"What are you doing?"

He began pulling me towards the den. "Come on."

I held my ground. "Stop this. Do you know what you're doing? You don't want to accept responsibility for anything that went wrong. What do you think, by putting me in my place you'll put your life in order?"

He tugged me a step further. "Move."

"No."

"Should I call the children?"

"You wouldn't," I said.

"Are you sure?" With his free hand he reached inside my robe. I tried to remove his hand from my breast but he was too strong for me.

He pinched the nipple and I cried out in pain. He released it. "You don't want me to hurt you, do you?" On the other side of his masculine disdain was his desire to care for the weaker sex. I had seen him baby Susan. I saw a sign, a fleeting look of remorse. "I'm going to take you, one way or the other tonight, Joan. Would you like me to gag you, maybe? Tie you up?"

"No."

We grappled with each other as he tried to pull off my robe.

155

"Get your hands off me!" I felt as though I were losing control. The touch of his hands was repelling.

I pulled the robe around my body as he let go of me to unzip his fly. The sight of his thickening organ, having no relationship to pleasure, alarmed me.

I was no match for him in strength. I had to do something. I found myself saying, "You're not circumsized, are you?"

Silence.

I double knotted the belt of my robe. "Come on, Roger. What's happening here?"

He hid the limpness with his hands.

"Susan loves you. Go home."

"I don't want you, you know," he grumbled, embarrassed.

After Roger left with his children, I lay in bed unable to sleep.

Under other circumstances, the touch of Roger's strong hands on my body might have been a pleasant sensation. Without volition, it had been a contamination. Self-ownership, my most inalienable right, had almost been lost, defined by its peril.

15

Two days later Stuart called, supposedly to say hello to John and Laura and set up a date to see them, but really to suggest that he and I "seek counselling." I told him of my encounter with Roger and he felt, I surmised, more than a smidgeon of responsibility. That, along with his weekend with Susan, served to balance the books for him, and he was ready to open a new account.

He wanted to talk to me, preferably where we wouldn't be bothered by people we knew. We excluded the house and his apartment for psychological reasons. I suggested Earl's, a restaurant-bar in Easthampton, as a neutral corner. He agreed.

I arrived a few minutes early and got us a table for two—the last empty one. The place was already bubbling over with personality and good cheer, the sounds of shared well-being, guffaws of appreciation, jokes well received. The young summer crowd was hanging over the bar, establishing new, reaffirming old, relationships. Friendly conversation, dinner and drink orders, introductions, buzzed around the tables, magnified by the low-beamed ceiling, lit up by the suspended Tiffanys. An aura of confidence—in looks, in loves, in Levis—hung in the air. Only a touch of frenzy in the gaiety, a note of frantic delight in the exhibitionism, in the competition.

I ordered a Bloody Mary from a girl in an aproned miniskirt, and tried not to feel isolated. At the next table, two young women, looking out of place and slightly agonized, were stirring their drinks with their celery sticks and evaluating their situation with furtive glances around the room. They tugged at the strings of my heart. They looked like two working girls—secretaries, perhaps—who had combined their savings in order to spend a week in the Hamptons. They probably had some nice qualities— maybe one was a terrific cook, one had a good head for figures— qualities that needed time to be discovered and enjoyed. But there was no *time* here, and it did not seem as though they had the manners that would gain them easy access. Certainly, they did not possess the beauty that would bring them gratuitous love. One had a weak chin and the other had bad teeth and mousy hair. Neither was the type who rides above her imperfections or shines through her discomfiture.

Stuart arrived as the waitress brought my drink. He appeared, as usual, neat and tidy, commercially handsome. The two girls noticed him and pretended not to.

"You're looking well, Stuart."

"Thanks. So are you." He frowned. "This place is extremely noisy. How are we supposed to talk here?"

"I can hear you fine."

The amenities out of the way, and the dinners served, we began talking seriously. "Perhaps," he suggested, picking at a piece of lobster, "if we were advised in disturbances of this nature . . ."

"Do you really want to discuss why I—"

"Stop. I don't want to hear about your indiscretion, if that's what you're about to bring up."

"Oh, Stuart, could we ever have anything more than a truce?"

Stuart stared at a point over my shoulder. He coughed. "I am willing to seek help and possibly make amends."

158

"We're supposed to be husband and wife, not two foreign countries," I sighed.

"What would you have me do, Joan?"

"Do? Nothing. It's not a question of pragmatics." My food looked unappetizing. I laid down my fork.

"If you had only been more self-disciplined. I am finding this up-in-the-air way of living very disconcerting, Joan. And I am sure the children are terribly confused."

"They're confused. But not terribly. They're doing okay. Really."

Stuart was bent over his food, absently spearing peas. His handsome face stared into his plate. At that moment the mental snapshot of Gil in his plaid robe, slumped over his footnotes, bare leg protruding, popped into view and stung my viscera like an arrow. With difficulty I suppressed the image and the pain.

"I don't know, Stuart. I have to get my bearings. You have to give me time."

"I can hardly hear myself think in this place."

One of the girls dropped her purse on the floor and its contents spilled out. She was embarrassed. I looked over at Stuart, as if reading his instinctive response to the accident would answer a question. There was no sympathy there. There was annoyance and—arrogance. I got down on the floor to help the girl retrieve her belongings.

Understanding through counselling? No. Stuart wanted to reeducate me. He would have me censured.

"Give me some time," I said again, later, over coffee.

"Until school starts?"

"Yes." (Oh, Susan, if we ever bump into each other in the soup aisle, don't turn away. I understand. We all want it. What is it we want? What is it we're looking for? It's so elusive.)

"Are you having more coffee?" he asked.

I left Earl's feeling very much alone. I wanted to see Gil. He would reach through—wouldn't he?—all the hurt and petulance, to touch and comfort without questions and answers. Even for just a *little* while? Forgetting history and game plan? He could—couldn't he?—reach across the gulf that kept me so lonely.

It was after ten when I knocked at his door. The look of innocent surprise quickly turned to wariness. "Come in," he said. "To what do I owe the honor?"

I stood by the open door. "I just came to say hello."

"Did I forget something? A canvas? A tube of paint? I thought I returned it all."

"Don't. I just came to . . . say hello."

"Well, hello."

"I thought . . . maybe you would have . . . called?"

"Look, Joan. I created a myth. It was exploded. I thought you were *mine*. I was wrong. I'm not a glutton for punishment. I wanted to avoid post mortems. Save you the trouble. Are you coming in?"

"Would you come for a walk along the beach, and not talk, or anything?"

He stood in the doorway, holding onto the knob. There was a hole in his sweater in the crook of his arm. "Why?"

"I'm feeling very down and lonely. It's as simple as that. Will you come?"

He sighed. "I'm serving a purpose again."

"Please—will you come? No questions? No admonitions? Just a plain old *walk*?"

"You'll be cold without a sweater. Are you cold?"

"No . . . Yes."

"Just a minute." He brought me one of his cable knits. "Put it on."

We drove to Dune Road in his car, saying nothing. He parked in the empty parking lot at Marlin's and we walked across the road, along the Club's desolate boardwalk, to the beach. The moon was full. The waves glistened. We had left our shoes on the boardwalk. The sand was cool.

We walked westward along the beach, side by side, listening to

160

the ocean. When we came to a jetty we climbed over it independently, and continued on alongside the water's edge. Without speaking.

He didn't break stride. He simply reached across the silence and took my hand as we walked. I didn't dare look up at his face. In a little while our hands began moving against each other. Our fingers were interweaving.

We reached another jetty and stood still. We embraced and sank to our knees. Holding on to each other, our cheeks touching, we began rocking together. Rocking, rocking. Who was the comforter?

We lay in the cool sand, cradling each other very closely, hardly moving, breathing against each other's faces. Closing the gulf. We were together without a kiss, drawing comfort and strength.

I don't know how long we lay there, but time doesn't stand still forever, except when you're dead. Finally, I spoke. "I guess we should go back."

"I guess so."

We rose and brushed the sand from our clothing. We walked back to the car, slowly, our arms around each other's waists.

"How *was* that party, anyway?" he asked, as we drove back to his cottage. "You know, the one I missed."

Why not be honest? "It was a little wild, after all."

"I thought so."

"You let the bird out of its cage and . . . well . . . the window was open."

"And you met Jonathan Livingston Seagull and off you went to the top of the mountain?"

"No. I've only been to the top of the mountain with you."

"It's a good line, Joan. Except we're not birds or metaphors. What you did, you did."

"And why or how doesn't matter to you, does it? You know, you're really a very pure man. You'd make a great saint. You'd make a lousy priest, though."

He parked near my car. I got out. I slipped off his sweater and gave it to him. I walked over to my door. He came too. "Aren't you coming into the house?"

"Maybe I'd better not," I said.

"It's home to the . . . hubby and the kids, then?"

"The kids. The hubby's moved out."

"Melodrama. She, tearfully begging him to return, the children, tugging at her skirts, the roast, burn—"

"Gil. Stop." I found my car keys. "Can't we wait? Stop and wait?" I opened the car door.

"Your loyalties are too complicated for me."

"I'm sorry." I got into my car.

He punched the window. "Aren't I going to get a piece of the action, too?"

I was not a glutton for punishment either. I had to get it into my thick head that the business of life could not be conducted on a moonlit patch of sand. I started the engine.

He thumped on the window. "I'm *sorry*! Get out of the car, for god's sake!"

I would not be owned. I would not be ordered. I would not— *could* not—become a package. I wasn't going to shut up and play dead for Stuart. I wasn't going to be a childless Cinderella for Gil.

I backed out of the driveway as Gil stood to one side. I didn't look into his face. I was afraid to.

I knew my limitations.

162

16

If I had made love to Gil after our walk on the beach, it would have been too difficult to break away, and I knew I had to. The men I had gone to bed with since my proclamation of independence were diversions. Those men, whom I met either through my job at Harrison's or at various parties I attended, did not interfere with my ability to function as a free woman. When Gil had entered me, he had inhabited my body and we lived in it together. Everyone else rented a room on the bottom floor of a house where I was the landlady. I could handle boarders.

Painting was more than a distraction. It devoured energy and essence and then filled me with even more.

Jeffrey had been right. Sally Nelson liked my canvases and asked me to take part in her August exhibit, along with two other local artists. For the moment, gratification eclipsed regrets at having no lover to share it with. I was forming, *experiencing* the substance of my singularity.

The morning after the opening reception, I went to the gallery to talk over the success of the event with Miss Nelson. While I was waiting for her to complete a telephone call in her office, I strolled through the exhibit pretending to be an objective tourist. As I was looking at one of my works from across the large sunlit room, and feeling another surprise sting of admiration, Susan walked into my field of vision. I hadn't spoken to her or seen her since the delivery of Bobby and Bill that fateful weekend.

She raised her hand carelessly as I hurried toward her. "Look what the cat dragged in," she slurred, opening her arms to display herself. "Thought I'd stop by for an autograph. Joan *Wolf,* isn't it?" She had been drinking.

"I'm glad you came by."

"I came by to take a look at these marrrrvelous works here!" She spread her arms and almost backed into a painting. She turned to examine it. "Say, this is terrific! And such a little autograph here in the corner for such a *colossal* thing. I'll take it! How much does it cost?"

"Maybe you should think it ov—"

"I want this picture. How much does it *cost*?" She began fumbling in her bag.

By this time Sally Nelson had come from her office. She smoothed the already smooth gray hair behind her ears and strode towards us. "May I be of some assistance?"

Susan pointed her finger at one of the dancer's heads. "Are you the owner here? What is the price of this?"

"Yes. The painting is eight hundred dol—"

"Sold!"

Susan sat down on the bench and found her checkbook. "Pen, anyone?"

Miss Nelson looked at me, raised her eyebrows, and went to fetch a pen.

"Are you *sure,* Susan?" I asked, touching her arm.

"I *want* it."

The pen was given to her and she made out a check, ripped it out of her book with a flourish, and gave it to Miss Nelson, who examined it.

Susan walked over to the painting—how I'd struggled to get that blue just right!—and began removing it from the wall. I rushed over to stop her. "No, no. It stays up until the show is over."

"How professional! Will someone sticker this as sold, please?"

164

As I realigned the canvas, I remembered how it had stood against the easel at Gil's, abandoned for days, incompleted, because I could see no way out of the linear confusion in the upper left quadrant.

"Where are you planning to hang it?" I asked, as Susan was rearranging the contents of her bag. "In your—"

Susan looked up at me, startled. "Are you kidding?" she cried. "I'm going to *burn* the fucking thing!" She slammed her bag shut. "What do you think of *that*?"

The impact was as physical as a blow to the chest. "No!"

"It's mine now. I can do whatever I want with it." She turned to Miss Nelson, whose mouth had dropped open. "You'll have this gift-wrapped for me, please?" She started to laugh, hysterically.

I planted myself in front of the painting.

"Where's the damn bathroom?" she uttered almost inaudibly, after she had caught her breath.

Miss Nelson led her to its door. I was an immovable fortress.

Miss Nelson returned. "Who *is* that woman?" she asked. I couldn't answer. "Don't worry, don't worry. She won't take it."

"Tear up the check!" I said.

"Let her do that herself."

"I've got to talk to her!" I ran to the ladies room, ready to do pattle with a woman who'd gone wild and hostile. I flung open the door. Ready for her attack.

Susan was slumped in a corner of the room, looking like a heap of dirty laundry on the clean white tiles. The smell was unbearable. The vomit was running down her blouse, pooled in her skirt. "Susan, oh, Susan!"

"Take me home," she whimpered.

Sally Nelson stuck her head in the doorway and gasped.

"Please go away," I said.

I opened the window. I took the blouse from her limp body and cleaned the front of it with paper toweling and water. I tried to clean her skirt with what was left of the toweling. Then I opened a fresh roll of toilet paper and wet a handful of it. I pressed it against her forehead. Wiped her face. "Susan. Oh, gee."

I put my arms around her.

165

"Take me home."

"Come." I helped her to her feet and got her blouse back on. She was a mess. "Can you walk to my car? It's right outside."

"I don't know."

"Try."

We stumbled out of the room. Passing Miss Nelson, I said, "I'm taking my friend home."

"Of course. Do you need help?" She was tearing up Susan's check.

"No."

We managed to get to the car. I belted her in. "You really are a mess," I said, hoping that she would see some humor in the situation, although I saw none myself.

"I sure am," she sighed.

All the way to her house, I exhorted her to take hold of herself, tried to get *through* to her in some way, offered to help her in some way—*what* way?—begged her to recall—recall? *find*, maybe, not recall—her self respect. "Do you want to come to my house now?" I asked. "Let's do that, okay? We'll talk?"

"Take me home."

I parked in her driveway. "Your car—I'll drive you to Bridge-hampton tomorrow—we'll pick it up. All right?"

"No. Roger will—NO!"

"I'll call you, then, tomor—"

"No."

She didn't want me. Crisis had severed us.

It was more than our tennis season that had come to an end.

17

A few times during August, Zenia had invited me to drop by the rental I had found for her and her friends, but I was either too busy or preferred to say I was. This time, however, I thought I caught the hint of a playful threat in her words.

"Don't you want to pick up the photos we made together, Joan honey?" she sang in her breathy, high-pitched voice. "On second look they're really quite good. And what do you think? They're doing a profile of me in *Playboy!*"

Was this simply a ruse to get me over there so that she could have another go at one of her contested conquests? Did she mean to have those photos published? My father, who tempted fate every month by leafing through a copy of *Playboy,* would surely not survive the issue! And what if one of John's or Laura's precocious little classmates recognized me? Did I want to be circulated in a clandestine period of Show and Tell?

I decided not to take any chances. I drove over to the house that evening, planning to satisfy myself that I was not to be published with my hand gingerly exploring Zenia, come what may.

It was a warm, breezy evening. The house which Zenia and her friends had rented for the month was a big old multigabled affair in South Bay. It was set back on a narrow side street—framed by an untidy hedge and cushioned in crabgrass and dandelions. Off to one side a row of empty children's swings squeaked in the bay breeze.

Although it was the largest house on the quiet street, it was not exhibitionist. The gray paint on its shingles had begun to peel, and at least two window panes on its second story needed to be replaced. A big friendly house in a small country town, it looked as though it might have contained one or two congenial ghosts.

Actually, during the school year the house creaked with the stomping of small children happily engaged in the process of learning. A progressive day nursery owned and operated by a young couple, certified teachers with modest ambitions, *Les Élèves* was, as a summer rental, a white elephant. For purposes of summer rental, the couple had furnished several upstairs rooms with a few bedroom necessities purchased at various yard sales and the Salvation Army. It had neither pool nor court nor beach-front location. It was surrounded by year-rounders, older inhabitants who feared the intrusion of City morality, group activity, and youth in general. They complained of the noisy schoolchildren and were apprehensive about summer hippies. The couple, parents as well as teachers, were themselves members of the community, and had borne the complaints with durable smiles.

I did not know with whom Zenia was sharing the rental. I had told her that "grouper" rentals were not tolerated by the zoning board. She had told me, with an offended sniffle, that although her friends could not afford an expensive rental, they were perfectly respectable. The house had not been rented in July and there being no other prospective clients for August, I gave it to her with some trepidation.

I stepped across the broad, hollow-sounding wooden porch and knocked at the front door. I was greeted by a small, freckle-faced young woman in yellow shorts and tank top vigorously chewing a wad of gum. A very intense get-to-the-heart-of-the-matter type. Her carrot red hair, fluffed about her head in a frizzy mass, added fire to the impression. "Hello!" her voice rang out as she bared a set of gleaming whites. "You must be Joan. C'mon in."

"Hi. Yes, I am. Is Zenia home?" I asked, sidling past her.

I had to wait for a bubble to form, enlarge, burst and be retrieved before I received an answer. "Sure!" she smiled up at me with those glorious teeth.

"And you're—?"

"Sorry. Pat McCarthy. ZENIA!"

I looked around, evaluating. The bright commercial tweed carpeting, installed throughout the sprawling main floor, was immaculate. The windows sparkled. The furniture was dusted. I was, frankly, surprised. "The place looks fantastic," I said.

"Chris does a good job."

She sure did. I wondered if she had Thursdays off. Presently Zenia, bountiful breasts bobbing freely, came tripping down the staircase. She was wearing a miniscule baby blue bikini, which set off her burnished skin. "Joan!" she cried. "I was just about to jump into the shower. I've been on the beach all day!" She embraced me as if I were a bosom buddy which maybe she thought I *should* be, blotting her perspiration on my clean white tee shirt. She glowed like polished mahogany. "I love the sun."

"Where's Chris?" asked Pat. "I'm *starving,* man."

"Getting the wash from the line, I think," said Zenia. "Oh, yes. Joan, you've got to have supper with us. We're having lasagne. Everything's ready. It only has to be stuck in the oven for a few minutes. Chris makes a *terrific* lasagna. The best!"

"No, no," I objected. "I really just came to pick up the—uh—photos. I thought my—um—husband would think they were a real gas." (How was I going to ask for the negatives?) "No supper, thanks."

But Zenia wouldn't take no for an answer, insisting that I sample Chris's sensational lasagne.

The rear screen door slammed shut and we moved towards the sound. We were standing in the center of the main schoolroom. Enter, upstage, a young Atlas, wearing an apron around his waist

169

and carrying a basket of sun-dried clothes. "Joan," said Zenia. "I'd like you to meet Chris."

"Hello," said Chris, smiling agreeably.

"Oh . . . hi!"

Pat vigorously chewed on her bubble gum. "I'm starving," she said.

"The oven is warming. Just let me fold this load before everything wrinkles," said Chris. "Okay?" he added respectfully.

"Of course, hon," said Zenia.

"Did you make those calls to Grace and Arnold?" called Pat to Mr. America as he was ascending the staircase.

"Yes, Pat." He turned. "They'll both be able to paint the sets next week."

"Cool. And those letters to the sponsors?"

"Got them out this morning. We need more stamps."

"Right."

"I'll go fix us some salad," said Zenia.

Pat watched Zenia's retreating figure with admiration. "A real doll," she said, energetically chewing. "Got talent, too. I just gotta convince her she's got more to herself than her body. She could really project character. A fleshed-out Diana Ross, that's what she'd be."

Zenia returned with a bump and a grind. "Love to get me in one of your little Off-Offs, wouldn't you, baby?"

"Sure would."

"I wouldn't remember my lines."

"Don't put y'self down, sister. I see through your coyness. You gotta have faith in the ol' gray matter." She tapped her skull.

"You work in the theater," I said.

"She's a real terror!" called Zenia, on the way back to the kitchen.

Pat smiled. "I'm a real together pussycat." She lodged her behind in one of the nursery school chairs and casually flung her legs over the sides. A few flaming red hairs curled out from beneath her yellow shorts. While she fondled her toes the sound of Zenia's mellifluous rendition of "I'm in the Mood for Love" drifted to us from the kitchen. "I manage a little place called The Machine Shop down on MacDougal Street in the Village."

"What an interesting name," I said.

"The place was a machine shop before I took it over."

"Oh."

"A theater-in-the-round. Very good for audience participation. We do a lot of freewheeling stuff, besides the usual run. I like to get the audience involved, y'know what I'm saying?" She clicked a back-bubble. "Get them feeling that art is life and life is art, y'know?"

"Yes. How nice. I'd love to see some of your work."

Pat smiled wryly. "Good. Maybe you'll loosen up. You seem like a nervous broad, if—"

"Yes, I know what you're saying." (Everything is relative. To Stuart, I was an undisciplined hippie. To Pat, an un-cool chick.) "You must do an awful lot of commuting—that is, if you're working on a production now." I watched the bubble burst.

"Mmmmm," she said, peeling the gum from her nose. "We're working on a coupla one-acts now. Won't be opening for another two weeks, though. I gotta have some of your sea and salt air or I'll dry up by October. A coupla guys are working at the Shop this week for me. They were here, lying around and getting themselves fat last week, so *they're* cool." She absently began stroking the underside of her thigh, pulling on the stray hairs.

I wondered just how many unrelated tenants there were, anyway, and shuddered to think what Harrison would say about the setup. "Is Chris one of your actors?"

"Chris is my guy Friday. He does *everything*. The kid likes to be taken care of—can't make any big decisions—but he's wrapped tight, very good at handling small responsibilities and bit parts. Speak of the devil," she said, as Chris trotted by on the way to the kitchen.

I perched on the edge of one of the children's tables and glanced down at my limbs, hugged by my faded jeans. Pat's hand was wandering in and out of her shorts. Chris came in to tell us that supper would be ready in ten minutes, and from the way he

171

stared at Pat's maneuvers, I could see that beneath his apron lay a set of heterosexual balls.

"Can't I help?" I asked.

The dark-haired vision of strength in servitude declined the offer, giving me a boyish once-over with his big brown eyes. A nice boy, happy in his work. Probably not much education or ambition.

Zenia, shortly, came humming in with a tray of salad bowls, plates and utensils. The knot in her bikini top had relaxed, revealing the upper edge of one of her nipples. "Supper's about ready," she sang, placing the tray on the table on which I was sitting. She smiled at me warmly, and then at Pat. Pat stuck her gum under the table and caught me grimacing.

The room was furnished with a conference table and chairs, and we moved to the more formal arrangement when Chris bustled in with his lasagne, returning to the kitchen to get a jug of red wine and glasses.

After our meal (the lasagne surpassed my expectations), Chris cleared the table and, again, I offered to help but was thwarted.

Zenia suggested we "light up" and her friends agreed. "We've got some really *super* pot—don't we, hon?"

"Yeah," said Pat, rising from the table. "Go roll us a couple, Chris. Not for you. The stuff makes you sick."

In a manner of speaking I had come a long way, but this was one trip I hadn't been on. I balked.

"You think we were asking you to throw us a snow job," Pat said gruffly.

Well, they said the lasagne would be good and—oh, why the hell not? What was that—"the flower that smiles today, tomorrow will be a-dying"?

Chris trotted upstairs and returned with a brown paper bag. "Let's go to the playroom," said Pat. "This room reminds me of my first grade teacher, Mrs. Wisterly. I don't think I could hang loose with *that* icy tit freezing the air."

Actually, the playroom did seem more suitable for a turn-on. It was furnished with a small jungle gym, a large crawl-through tube, called a "caterpillar," and two floor mats. Chris pulled down the blinds and lit a lamp in the corner of the room. He placed an ashtray on one of the mats. The four of us sat on a mat, and Chris lit a hand-rolled cigarette for us.

Zenia delicately inhaled. I recognized the aroma. But from where or when? In the high school locker room that time I took John to a basketball game? On the ferry to Sag Harbor when I went *below* to buy a bag of potato chips? In the public toilet at Penn Station? "Have a drag," Pat prodded, and took one herself.

"Just put it up front, lightly between your teeth and take a small draw," instructed Zenia. "Try to let the smoke out your nose." I tried it and waited for the unexpected. The taste was mildly pleasant, but not intoxicating. Nothing. Chris was dutifully massaging a crick out of Pat's neck. Zenia's nipple was now fully exposed. I took another puff. Hmmm. . . . By the third or fourth drag I was beginning to feel the effects. Light-headed and off center. A little later the symptoms became more, as the room became less, defined, the wine I had drunk perhaps adding to my condition. Perspectives and angles of planes shifted. Gravity became a factor to be reckoned with as the floor tilted. Some images became fuzzy as others became clearer, as if a camera were being focused. Zenia's face blurred as the shades of her nipple became microscopically clear. Her nipple faded into the background as her eye became a lake of variegated browns and ochres, dappled with flecks of algae and anima. I felt soft and friendly and free, and yet in a corner of my mind I felt the presence of a cool surveyor, clear-headed and aloof, sifting out images and by-play.

I remember discontinuous fragments of what followed.

Pat is standing above us. A narrow beam of light from between the slats hits her curly mop of red, forming a halo. She grins and the angel becomes fiery Satan, head aflame. "I got a great idea for a Shop scene." She drifts over to the caterpillar. "You walk through this thing and presto—when you come out the other side you're transformed into what you always wanted to be. No holds barred. What an outlet for draftees from the audience!" Zenia rises from the mat. "Let's go." They crawl into the tube, one behind the other. There is some scuffling. They emerge on the other side. They are naked—earth and fire.

"Here we are," croons Zenia.

"In a brave new world," adds Pat.

"Right on!"

Chris retrieves the clothing from inside the caterpillar. He hangs it neatly on a rung of the jungle gym.

I am standing. I find it hard to keep my balance because the floor is tilting. Zenia's eyes are burrowing into me. I look down at my white tee shirt. My breasts seem unusually large. I am the angel in white, accessible and alluring. I raise my arms. The cool witness is watching and waiting. "I wish—" I falter. The wish is on the tip of my tongue. "I wish I could float away in a bubble with . . ." I think of Pat's bubble growing larger and larger . . . "to whisk, to whisper off beyond the edge of time with . . ." I cannot say his name here . . . "With . . ." I have had this wish before, a million light years ago, before the summer began. I sit back down on the mat, unsettled.

Zenia is splayed out on a mat. I am smearing her with finger paints. She opens her legs still wider. I apply a daub of bright yellow between her legs, smoothing it up into her creamy cleft. I massage and probe as her purple mountains heave. She groans loudly and I can feel her tinted walls twitching against my fingers. I continue to rub, reaching up further. She cries out as the walls begin another series of contractions, this time stronger, pulling me deeper inside. The boa is ingesting me, slowly. Chris is holding her head in his lap, brushing her hair away from her face.

Rick Wakeman's *Six Wives of Henry VIII* (one of my favorites—remember Stuart's frown of distaste?) is going full blast on the nursery phonograph. The universe is filled with the resounding strains of Moog and Mellotron depicting the fate of Anne of Cleves.

I am drawn to Chris, he is so lovely to look at. I am helping him off with his clothes, unwrapping a god, or is he a satyr? No, he is a beautiful, tame beast, whose paws roam my body, whose face I do not see. I am not looking for faces. Only bellies, legs. My own, encased in clothing, must be bared. We strip my body and now we are all beasts. It is to the one with a projection between his legs that I am drawn.

I am lying on my back, the red mane of the lioness is nearing that aching place between my legs—there. She sucks in on the wound, appeasing, as the sleek-skinned creature ranges over my breasts and belly, leaving wet patches where her tongue meets my flesh. The tame beast crouches over my face, his organ brushing my lips. My tongue touches its tip. I go to stroke it, to guide it into my mouth. There are animal sounds. Mine.

The music is loud and bass, vibrating the room. The change, automatic; the beat is rock now. Zenia and Pat are moving my limp body—I have made myself limp for them—moving it onto Chris. They move me about until I am placed just so, my legs spread apart, my arms raised above my head. I help as they hitch me onto his organ. He comes to life in a frenzy of movement beneath my body, grabbing my rear and pushing it against his pelvis, rotating and thrusting against me. Zenia's hands are wedged between my chest and his, squeezing my breasts. Pat is stroking my arms and legs. I begin to feel a deep stir. It is mushrooming, swelling up from the depths of my belly, towards the void. From beyond the point of deepest penetration it is coming, and coming. I am tossed by the body beneath me, whose projectile suddenly begins a tremendous spasmatic release inside me.

My chamber pulsates and throbs with a life of its own. Pure sensation—neural, muscular.

Memory becomes continuous. I lay there, worn out. The music was blaring on. Nearby, Zenia and Pat were joined, their faces buried between each other's legs. I looked down into Chris's face, awed by the fact that he was a total stranger. My stomach growled, hungry again.

Sitting alone on a mat, I felt afraid of becoming swept into the loud rock music filling the room with its insistent beat.

Huddled there on the floor, I suffered the same fear of loss that I had experienced with Roger when he threatened to sever volition from deed. Only this time it was my doing. I had squandered something of myself.

There was a growing awareness that I had violated myself, that I had gone from freedom to fragmentation. Will there be a time when stimulus and response will be all-important, and even gender will be superfluous? The child in me was alone and forlorn. The woman was out on a limb.

I remembered how it was afterwards, with Gil. How orgasmic rhythm would billow into my thoughts, sometimes so expansive that I would think there had to be a God because where, if not in Him, could such a plexus of physical and mental joy be contained?

Here, a dichotomy of thought and matter.

I was afraid. Not of the hand of the devil, but of my own anarchy. I had freed my sexuality with Gil and it had enabled me to express the deepest part of my nature. Was it detaching itself from me, threatening to run rampant, to trample what it had nurtured? What would happen to me?

My painting, now the healthiest part of me—would its soul-spark go out, leaving me with style only? I looked down at my nakedness and closed my eyes. I could see a portrait of stylized decadence, in black and white, like a Beardsley. A woman seated at her vanity. Grotesquely large breasts. A look of contempt. At her side, an enormous penis, extending from between the legs of a courtier. The portrait bordered by an ornate garland of lifeless flowers.

At that moment I made a choice as well as a judgment. I don't like it here. I shouldn't be here.

But what *was* that? What did I hear in the pauses between musical thrusts?

Chris turned off the phonograph. Someone was loudly knocking on the door. Pat tore herself away from Zenia, and rushed to a window. Peering out between two slats, she whispered hoarsely, "Jesus, it's a police car!"

What to do first. Get dressed. Act fast.

"Hide the stuff!" Pat ordered.

"Easy, hon." Zenia touched Pat's thigh. "It's not as if we were taking a powder."

"We're in the sticks now. Grass is bad enough."

There was another knock. "Hello there! Police! Open up, please!"

It is amazing what can be accomplished in ninety seconds. Lights were lit. Finger paints, blotted from Zenia, were washed from faces. Clothing was thrown on bodies. Except for Zenia's. She, naked, scooped up the evidence and fled upstairs, not before spraying the room with lemon scented furniture polish and grabbing a container of chopped liver from the refrigerator.

"Yes?" I asked, terrified, as I opened the front door. I was wearing Pat's yellow tank top. I pushed my underpants deeper into the pocket of my jeans.

The two officers stepped into the house and my heart sank. Unexpected confrontation of spheres: the one with the mole on his cheek was John's Cub Scout leader. He looked surprised. "Why, hello Mrs. Hiller," he said. "We're here on a neighbor's complaint."

"Hello, Bert." I felt weak. Pat and Chris stood near.

Bert coughed. "We got a call from the neighbors. They complained about the loud music."

Just then the complainants came striding up the path, onto the porch and into the house. The man might easily have been an officer of the Rotary Club; the woman, coiffed and polyestered, a tender of gladioli. They were fuming, in a state of double-chinned resentment.

"Who the hell *are* these hippies, anyway?" the man blustered. "We don't allow groupers here, you know? Especially *deaf* ones!" He looked around. "Where are the rest of them? I know there are more of them!"

"I am visiting this family," I started to explain to Bert.

177

"Kissing cousins, I imagine," sneered the woman.

The front door still ajar, the sea smell drifted to us from the shore. Pat explained that she and her husband (a convincingly loving smile from Chris) were celebrating their second anniversary. She said she was sorry about the music being so loud. The twosome was appeased only when it learned that the perpetrators were vacating the premises within a few days.

Our visitors left, tut-tutting but mollified, and Pat slammed the door behind them. I was inordinately grateful at having avoided imprisonment, a life of degradation, worse.

Pat and I exchanged shirts and Zenia ("Coast clear, gang?") reemerged in a diaphanous mumu, carrying an empty chopped liver container ("There are times my diet just won't stick!") and a manila envelope. She asked me to stay for a snack of crackers and cheese. I wanted to go home to John and Laura with a hunger stronger than what I felt in my stomach. I said no.

Zenia smiled. "It was nice that you came." She extended the hand containing the manila envelope. "Don't forget your photos."

"And negatives for the paranoia," added Pat.

I reached for the envelope. "Thank you," I said.

Zenia smiled wistfully. "And give my regards to your husband." I flinched. "I'm sorry I never met him." She touched my shoulder tenderly.

I opened the door. "It was nice . . . meeting you," I said, looking at Pat and Chris.

"Thank you," said Chris. "You, too."

"You're letting the bugs in," said Pat.

The earth was stable but I was still echoing with its tremors. I needed to hold my children very badly. "Goodbye," I said, letting go of the door and running off into the night with my legal-sized manila envelope and a sudden urge to cry like a goddamn baby.

In the semidarkness of her room, I crept into bed with sweet Laura, under the Sesame sheet. Her fine brown hair was fanned out over Big Bird. Her delicate chest was uncovered, for coolness. In her sleep she was turned toward the wall, presenting me with her warm back, her softly rounded calves, the smooth soles of her feet. I tucked up against her, feeling her through the sheer fabric of my nightgown. The touch elicited feelings so different from those sensual eruptions caused by the friction of Gil's body against mine. Alike only in that the stimulus reverberated through my body, affecting the total perception of myself and the other.

Now, up against sweet Laura, it was as though my womb were invaginating, the outside of my body becoming a tender cavity to house without bruising its ripened fruit. Oh, my delicious baby, lovely soft shoulder, soft round pantied hiny, tiny sun-tipped nose I reached around to touch with my fingertip.

Closeness made child remembrances, unthinking needs, surface. I could feel the irrational love-blanket, niceness of new skin against powdered mommy, furry daddy. I was parent and child. Only with Gil, in tender moments, had I felt anything comparable to this dual-roled commingling. Oh Laura love, I need to be taken care of, too. I held her close and drifted off to sleep in an aura of sweet smelling shampoo.

I am running through the Vassar Library stacks, peering into study cubicles, looking for a book on Hegel's dialectic which I am responsible for but which I can't remember having read. In fact, I can't remember having attended any of the classes in Modern Philosophy, but I am about to take a final exam. If I don't pass I will not get the three points credit I need to graduate and I will have to come back for another year and be mortified. I can't find the book. I am running around the grassy campus in my black cable-knit turtleneck, my sawed off jeans, my worn-out black ballet slippers. I come to a halt in the middle of a quad—Jocelyn is on my right, Strong on my left (I think). I am trying to remember what Mr. B. stressed about Hegel, but all I can remember is Mr. B's capped teeth. I try to make a schematic diagram of the jargon in my mind—logical analysis, infinite collection, ontological proof, mental auscultation—but all I can think about is forgetting and failing. I have forgotten the questions, no less the answers, that hounded me just a short time ago. About epistemology, existence, postivism, keys to the universe. My old dancing teacher marches into the quad and asks me to perform, but my body is stiff and for the life of me I can't remember what those mumbled French directives stand for. She struts off in disgust and I am left standing in the quadrangle trying to remember my best friend Marcia-from-first-grade's last name. I've got myself by the short hairs, quizzing myself away, and flunking, flunking. Not remembering. My father's face is fading. I can't remember what his voice sounds like. I can't remember exactly what it's like to change diapers, to heat up a baby food jar, how to spell Milton's Areo-Ario-Areopagitica?. I start running around in the quad, not knowing which dorms are which. Not remembering where I fit in, what number my room is, where or on what the test is being given. I'm all alone, in a solipsistic muddle, flunking. Who am I? What have I become? Where does the world begin? I'm in a huddle, a heap, in the dark. Then into the darkness, like a bubble in a cartoon, comes a lit-up memory. A palpable exerpt. I am thirteen years old. I am asking my mother if she would be willing to die if she could find out the secrets of the universe and all the reasons for things as they are. She says no and I am aghast. I slam the door to the bathroom and from within I yell out to her, "If it's not learning the truth about things, then what do you think is the most important thing about life?" She raises her voice, only in order to be heard. "To be happy!" What? "I want to be happy and I want you to be happy." I sit down on the bathroom floor, not believing that she's actually mouthed this simplistic answer. The quad is dark and I'm sitting in a heap on the cold grass. I feel a book next to me. I open it up. It is dark, but I can see the pictures through my fingers. I see the picture of a Jew being beaten on the head as an experiment in brain damage as it relates to ambulation. I see the pictures of scrawny dead Jews, once vessels of hope and animation, piled high in layers of disposal. Is there some-one there in that heap with a particular mouth like mine, inherited from a common cousin? I am feeling the excruciating dread of death as though I were seven and slipping from the center of the universe. I am thinking of my grandfather comforting me: "Joan, sweetheart, I'm much older than you and I'm going to die way before you do and I'm not afraid." Another memory intact. The quad is dark and the exam, I think, may be over. I'm thinking—maybe I already took that test on Modern Philosophy. In my junior year, maybe. A ray of light shines down from a room high up in Jocelyn (or is it Strong?). Some crammer is shedding a ray of light, or it is hope?

I woke up as the dawn was breaking. I was desperate to touch the elusive pulp of another human being and to celebrate the existence, albeit temporary, of my own. I kissed Laura's soft shoulder, her young back. Be happy. Be happy. Be happy, my baby.

Oh, how I wished I had a man to hold me until death do us part.

18

Where was my future, my "drummer," then? Neither at the Sheik, the disco at one end of Hampton Village, nor the Country Club at the other. Neither controting to the percussive ear-splitting sounds with the chick-hunting colorfuls, the mix and match couples, nor stepping to the tired baton with the pink and mint-green ladies in pants suits and their men in white pants, white shoes, white hair, white dreams. I didn't belong with the swinging minglers or the placid flaccids. I wasn't a hip hedonist, but neither did I intend to mark time for the rest of my life. Too square to find ecstasy in total freedom. Too rounded to find contentment in security as an end in itself.

At the beginning of September I attended Gloria's wedding and declined, amid the mauve heroines and tearful relatives, to renew the vows with Stuart. But then, I wanted someone to hold my head if I puked, hold my hand if I had a breast amputated, feel my grief if my father suffered a stroke. I wanted the comforting boredom of commitment, the limited martyrdom of faithfulness, the sweet predictability, and with it, the steady fuck, forever a voluptuous surprise.

Plus ça change, plus c'est la même chose. Almost. I was nevermore going to "settle." I could adapt my needs; I would not mask my identity. I could deprive myself of my whims; I would not stifle my deepest desires.

And what would I tell Stuart? Our talk was about due. That it was better to be sorry than safe? That we could not regain what we had never lost? That he was like the moon affecting the temporal tides, but what I wanted was the sun to warm the sea of life?

I'd think of something.

It was September 10th. My meeting with Stuart was scheduled for the 11th. The day before I had gone into the City to deliver a completed series of illustrations to Jeffrey Kane, who was pleased, eager to begin another project soon. I had also called Gladys to tell her that I was looking for a fall replacement. "What?" she exclaimed. "Your game will just go to the dogs!"

I didn't tell her that I was taking precautions in case that should turn out to be my financial state, but did explain that my schedule was going to be erratic and full. "I'll be happy to substitute when I can, or keep in touch with an occasional game of singles." I would miss those scheduled confrontations. There was no doubt about that.

"What about Susan? She dropping out, too?" I could feel myself blush. "I don't know. I haven't spoken to her for awhile. You better call her."

September 10th. The death throes of summer, epitomized by the frantic activity of the Labor Day weekend, had come to an end. Some of the stylish windows on Main Street and its modish mews would soon be emptied, displaying See you in the Spring! signs. Other stores, with the precious lower-case names, would be noting, on their doorways, that they would be open weekends only. Then, after awhile, this routine would peter out and we would again be left with staples like Gristede's Supermarket and Stern's Department Store to supply us through another winter of minimal activity and maximal parking. Landlords would be surveying the damages, determining whether or not they were justified in keeping their extra months' securities. Summering land-owners would be clearing out and locking up, a few perhaps debating the practicalities of staying and commuting to work this year. Mr. Harrison would be cleaning his desk, as he always did at the end of the summer season, and begin concentrating more on local movement and development, the rise and fall of families moving up and into or retiring and vacating. The fair grounds on Montauk Highway would be bare—without tents, antique autos and tilt-a-whirls—for another year. Dune Road was being returned to the elements and the few die-hard year-round residents and stragglers. The high school tennis courts were being returned, by the summer hackers, to the lean youths in green and white, striving for another successful year of team competition. Children's bathing suits were being stored. New clothes and school jitters were coming out of the closet as bedtime schedules were being revised. Bathhouse lockers were being emptied, cleared of sea-smelly towels, sagging rafts, sandy caps.

It was a cloudy, cool afternoon. I was sitting on the beach in my usual, most convenient spot, across from the Marlin parking lot, in my rolled up dungarees and an old Mexican blouse. My hair, badly in need of a cut, was blowing about my cheeks and into my eyes. I was trying to reread an old college textbook, Philipp Frank's *Philosophy of Science,* pausing in wonderment over my obtuse marginal notes, and trying to instruct and discipline my children in the art of flying a kite at the same time. Aside from an occasional beach jogger, we were alone.

"Mommy!" Laura called, and I looked up for the fiftieth time. "John is ruining it! He's not letting go of the kite when a good breeze comes!"

"Let go of the kite when a good breeze comes along," I urged John. "And Laura, you try to let the string unwind faster, too, when John lets go."

I went back to my book:

> To give a simple example: in the case of the hydrogen atom, the
> only orbits that are compatible with the observed spectral lines are

those whose angular momentum is an integral multiple of a certain constant that is equal to $h/2\pi$, where h is Planck's constant, which occurred in the previous Section in the expression for the energy of a light quantum of the frequency v. This energy hv is observable in the photoelectric effect, and, therefore, h can be calculated.

My marginal response fourteen years ago had been an assertive fat-nibbed "YES!" Now it was a quizzical "'Simple'??" I wondered if there were some condition akin to charley horse of the brain. If so, I'd have it tomorrow.

After another taxing paragraph I looked up. Laura was furiously letting out string as the serpentine kite was rising above the frivolous breezes towards the coasting winds. "Yay!" cried John, jumping up and down. "There it goes!"

"Remember, I hold the string for three whole minutes!" warned Laura, firmly planted in the sand, clutching the spool.

"Terrific!" I called. "Just don't fight. And I get a turn, too, you know!"

"How about me?" asked a familiar voice from behind. "Do I get a turn?"

"Sure," I answered at once, avoiding the pregnant pause. When I turned I could see the line of his footprints coming down from the Marlin's deck. "After me."

Gil was wearing his summer khakis and a white, short sleeved button-down, open at the neck. His hair was wind-flipping across his forehead. He made me think of a boarding school boy, home for the holidays. He plunked down awkwardly at my side.

"So . . . are we just bumping into each other?" I asked, concentrating on the suspended kite.

"No. I called Harrison's. His secretary told me you might be here with the kids."

"Why did you look for me?"

"I just sent the bibliography to the publisher this morning. The book's officially finished."

"That's wonderful, Gil!—You mean you just drove out here from the City? Just like that?"

"It seemed like the thing to do."

186

Could he be publishing *and* perishing? I began playing with a page corner of my book. "Your schedule all set for the fall?"

"Classes began yesterday. How are *you* doing? Uh . . . painting? You . . . *should* be."

"Yes, I am." I folded the corner of the page.

"What are you reading?" He leaned towards the book, peering through his wire-rims, dangerously close. "Ah, looks like you're airing out the old ivory tower."

I smiled.

"Retreating or reviewing?"

"Refreshing."

"You look good."

"I'm trying to sort things out."

"Seeing how the sectors mesh? P.T.A., C.P.A., duty, pleasure, achievement sort of thing?"

"I guess."

"I can't see you becoming one of the totally self-absorbed careerists, anyway."

I didn't want to become subservient to either my clitoris or my ambition. Nor did I want to become a woman who so vehemently steels herself against exploitation and repression that, mistaking vulnerability for disability, she loses her humanity in the process. "Do you mean become a success-crazed bitch?"

"Yes."

"Never mind the monomania. Can you see me with a time consuming, independent commitment? Because there's a difference between the mad passion for status and the desire to be productive."

"Sure I can."

"But I don't think you'd like your mate going off on a tangent like that. You'd want to be the inspiration of her every serious pursuit. Of her every—"

"Still life with apples and bananas?"

"Yes." I sifted the cool sand through my fingers.

"I've changed."

"Just like that?"

"Your absence matured me."

"Maybe giving birth to a baby of your own—your book—matured you."

"Maybe that helped." He grinned. "You're keen on defining and evaluating, aren't you?"

"It must come from having had too many fireside chats with my father about Will Durant."

"You think maybe you went too far—testing theories, that is?"

(He means have I been screwing around indiscriminately. I've gone beyond my old fantasy, at least. That's a start, anyway—to be able to differentiate between pleasure and promise.) "I've had what you might call a baptism of fire," I said.

"You've been reborn?"

"I can make choices. When it comes to choosing the play—and the players."

"I see—I *am* beginning to see, you know. I'm just a slow learner."

"Your jealous furies. Over? Just like that?"

"It's taking an effort," he said.

"Supreme, I would think."

"Yes," he admitted.

"And is all the rage just—repressed?"

"I don't think so. I'm trying to reason it out. It's just too . . . important that I understand." He looked towards the children. "Do you know that you can send a message up the string to a kite?"

"No."

"Do you have a blank piece of paper?"

I carried a pad in my bag. I tore a page from it. He accidentally bumped my arm as he took the paper from me. "Sorry," he said. He bent towards me. "It . . . we . . . *will* persist, Joan." The shock of tenderness radiated from the place where his lips touched my cheek. From between my legs, where love pools, issued the hope that he was right.

In terms of independence, self-sufficiency, singularity, resilience, I was still a fledgling. I needed more time to feel my own strength, to determine my own moves before considering a binding commitment. But the sanctity of the self was one thing; isolation, another. Without yielding to the absurdity of romantic love I think my spirit would become rigid. I could never become a zealot of independence and the cathartic fuck. I had tested the limits of sexual variation and it had quickly begun to cloy.

What could I do? I still seemed to cling to the idea of the Definitive Love. There was a change, though. Now that I was becoming self-generative, I didn't need Gil or another man to give meaning to my life, but to augment it. I clung, but not tenaciously. A shotgun wedding was not in order. I could afford to step back and judge. Had Gil really come to terms with his possessiveness or was his adjustment as unstable as a New Year's resolution? Time would tell. In his favor, I hoped.

Gil took off his shoes and socks and put them next to my clogs. I put my book into my big straw bag and we stood up and walked closer to the water's edge, where the children were arguing about the measurement of time.

"You had three minutes!" John was saying. "You cheated!"

"I did not! The way you're supposed to count seconds is *one* one thousand . . . *two* one thousand . . . *three*—"

"See? You're too slow!" John turned towards us. "*Isn't* she?"

"I think maybe just a little," I said.

"I am not!"

"Let me introduce you to a friend of mine," I said. "Gil Ramsey. This is John, and Laura."

"Hello," said John. "Do you have a watch with a second hand?"

"I don't. But I *do* have a trick I bet you don't know. Can you send a message up the string to the kite?"

"No," said Laura, holding onto the spool tightly. A wave ended at her feet. Her little toes were curling into the wet sand. "How do you do that?"

"First tell me what message you want me to send up. Or maybe a wish?"

"Um—that I hope Miss Porter—she's my new teacher—is not

going to turn out to be mean like Carol Ann says she is and um—that there won't be any rain on my birthday so I can have my party outside."

"How about shortening it up to 'Be good Miss P and sun on Laura's B day'?"

"Okay."

Gil took a pencil from his shirt pocket and, resting the paper on John's shoulder, printed her message. "And yours, John?"

I regarded the three of them. I couldn't resist the temptation to think of them as father, son, and daughter. My affection for each of them sprang from the same source and made it easy to link them together. Stuart's jawline became an imposition on John's face. My feelings were stronger than that accident of fate. How soothing and fine that moment was.

"Coast clear agent number one," John recited.

"Sounds like top secret," Gil said. He recorded it. Then he wrote something else. "You finish it," he told me.

" 'M31+M32= . . .' " I remembered and smiled. They were the galaxy and nebula numbers we had used in our cryptic love notes.

"What's that?" asked John.

"Another top secret," replied Gil.

John looked questioningly up at Gil and as their eyes met I could see Gil try to hold his gaze for a few seconds, as if he were trying to acquaint himself, or force an exchange with John—of information or friendship. That look. He was trying. After all my explorations, exploitations, panting, and pulsations, I was a virgin again.

Still, I finished the equation with a simple question mark and my uncertainty was real, not coy.

"Launch time," I said.

Gil very carefully pushed the spool through the paper. "The winds will carry the paper up along the string to the kite. You'll see."

"Hey, neat!" exclaimed Laura, watching the paper slowly begin its ascent.

"Look at it go!" cried John. "Let me hold it now!" Surprisingly, Laura gave the spool to him without so much as a pout.

We watched the paper as it rose higher and higher, carried by the gentle winds, all of us concentrating on our messages floating up into the sky.

Was I like the kite, flying high, establishing the perimeters of liberty? How much string did I need, how much wanton breeze? "Hold onto the spool, John. Don't let go," I said.

"Hey, look, it's halfway there!" cried John. He started running with the kite. The rest of us followed in close pursuit.

We all ran along the beach, our prints marking the smooth wet sand, weaving and interweaving. Laura fell behind and Gil scooped her up in his arms and lifted her to his shoulders. She squealed with delight.

The waves roared towards us, bubbling and foaming, ending in a docile wash. I ran ahead of the group. I felt as though I could run and run without tiring—determining my own path. The air was cool. My hair was blowing into my face. The ties from my blouse were bobbing on my chest. The waves were cresting and foaming, approaching, forming again, washing the moment clean.

I could hear the giggling and squealing behind me, mingling with the sound of the waves.

I was running one step ahead of my future.